THE MYSTERY OF THE THIRD TWIN

THE MYSTERY OF THE THIRD TWIN

Wilma L. Yeo

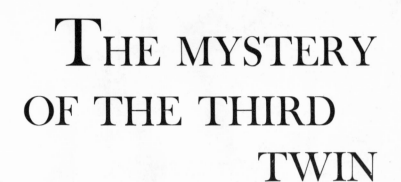

Illustrated by
Judith Gwyn Brown

SIMON AND SCHUSTER   NEW YORK

For Marli and Marji and Sandy
and in memory of Jack

CONTENTS

THE MYSTERIOUS "SHE"

Jinky leaned against the bare window and looked long-ingly at the sunny yard below. On any other morning as nice as this she would have been down on the sand-lot playing baseball with her team, the Indians.

But this was not an ordinary morning. This was the day the Smith family—Jinky, her twin sister Molly, and their mother and father—were moving to Nags Head.

The worst part of it all, Jinky thought, ramming her hands into her jeans pockets, is that spooky house we're going to live in when we get there.

She turned and scowled at the room that had once been a happy jumble of her things and Molly's. At least her own things had been a happy jumble—Molly's were always in touch-me-not order. Now the whole room was empty as an echo. Just as well go downstairs, she decided, and see what Molly's doing.

Jinky started down the hall, but had barely passed

her parents' half-closed bedroom door when she heard her father's voice, lowered to an unusual whisper. "I hope we're doing the right thing," he was saying, "keeping this a secret from Jinky and Molly until the investigation is complete."

Secret? Jinky skidded to a stop and backtracked two steps. Even though she'd been warned never to eavesdrop again, she leaned closer to their door. What did Father mean?

Jinky held her breath so she could hear her mother answer softly, "I *know* it's best not to tell the girls yet, even though we're going to need their help desperately—particularly Jinky's. After all, a lot depends on what we hear from Edward Scott."

Jinky's knees felt wobbly as a puppet's. She rubbed her sweaty palms down her jeans. Need *my* help? she wondered. And who's Edward Scott?

Whatever the secret is, she decided, edging closer to the crack in the door, Molly doesn't know about it either.

Now Father was saying, "Maybe Edward Scott will track down some information. If you'd seen her, you'd know we need all the help we can get."

Seen who? Jinky was so curious she took a chance on getting caught by peeping into her parents' room.

She blinked at the sunshine that poured through the bare windows. She had always thought this room was the prettiest in their house, but it seemed boxlike now. An ugly crack like a streak of lightning jagged across the wall behind Father. He had his carved hickory cane in one hand and his pipe, unlighted as usual, in the other.

Mother was hastily putting the last of her clothes into her suitcase. Jinky noticed that Mother's hands trembled as she folded her pink robe. "As soon as I've seen her, too," she said, "and learned more about the case, I'll know how to explain to Jinky and—" She stopped, raised a warning finger, and glanced toward the hall.

Jinky ducked back, but too late, because Mother called, "Who's there?"

Jinky was torn between walking away and pretending she didn't hear, or answering and acting as if she didn't know anything was wrong.

Finally she faked innocence, went inside, and asked, "Did you call me?"

"Jean Katherine Smith," Mother said, "how many times have I warned you not to hide around corners listening in on people!"

Jinky turned to make sure Father wouldn't see her cross her fingers behind her back. "I wasn't listening in," she said. *Why was it easier to fib than tell the truth when you were in trouble?*

The way Mother looked at Father said plainer than words, "Do you think we can believe her?"

Jinky stared down at the floor. But she had to look up sometime, and when she did, the expression on both her parents' faces sent worry wiggles through her mind. Pete's sake, she thought, that secret must be terribly important.

Mother poked the robe into the suitcase. "Your father and I are discussing something private, so you run along now."

Jinky knew she should be glad to get off so easily, but she wasn't—really. She left the room slowly, hoping they would call her back.

If they call me back, Jinky planned, I'll admit I eavesdropped. If I'm honest, maybe they'll tell me what the secret is. It has something to do with our moving, that's for sure.

Weeks ago Mother had explained to both her and Molly that moving to Nags Head would have "several advantages." Still, Jinky recalled now, she didn't say they were the *reasons* they were moving. She just said the ocean air would be good for Father, and that living in Nags Head would make it easier for him to do the research for his next book.

"Father's new book," Mother had said, "is going to be about a girl who lived long ago—a girl who disappeared mysteriously. Her name was Virginia Dare."

Of course, *Molly* had said that *she* knew all about Virginia Dare. "She was the first white child born in America," Molly had informed Jinky.

"I know who she was!" Jinky had said, even though she didn't.

At least I know one thing that Molly doesn't, Jinky thought, and it's that there is something very mysterious about our moving to Nags Head. But I suppose since I eavesdropped it would be wrong to tell Molly what I heard. Jinky looked back over her shoulder toward her parents' room.

Because she wasn't watching where she was going, she bumped smack into a packing crate stacked with things from the den.

She grabbed her throbbing knee with one hand and caught Father's teetering world globe with the other. When the globe stopped rocking, she saw that the pink rectangle of their state, North Carolina, was right under her hand. And there was the dot that marked this very town—Centerville—the only place she'd ever lived, the only place she ever wanted to live!

With a mixture of resentment and sadness she covered the dot with the tip of her pointing finger.

She moved her finger the rest of the way across the state to the blue Atlantic Ocean, then halfway down that little tail of land hanging out into the water of Albemarle Sound, to the dot marked Nags Head.

"Nags Head! Wags Head!" she whispered fiercely and sent all the blue waters and all the different-colored countries spinning in a dizzy blur.

Jinky looked once more toward her parents' bedroom, then started slowly down the steps.

She could hear the voices of the moving men coming up from the front porch. Maybe Molly was out there watching them.

Before breakfast the men had backed the big van up to the house and swung the heavy doors wide. As soon as the men went in the house to start packing things, Jinky walked the wooden ramp they had laid from the porch to the floor of the truck.

The inside of the van was like an empty room with a splintery floor and no windows then.

Now, as Jinky reached the bottom step, she saw through the propped-open door that it was more than half full of their furniture—some of it padded and roped like fat belted prisoners.

Her ball glove was lying on a box near the door. She snatched it up. Nobody was putting *this* in that moving van!

She put on her glove, pounded her fist into its smooth pocket, and whispered her team's password, "Poohw raw." It was her goobye to the Indians. She'd had to prove she could pitch better than any boy before the Indians finally let her on the team. They had made her swear she would never tell what poohw raw meant.

I never have told, Jinky thought, and I never will —not even Molly. "Poohw raw," she whispered again as she went out onto the front porch.

Molly was not out there. Pretending not to notice the moving men, Jinky dashed across the porch and recklessly jumped the rail at the far end.

Her heels dug hard into the sandy ground below, and she imagined the men were saying to each other that she was a mighty good jumper for a girl.

She kept thinking this all the way to the back yard, because it warmed her mind like hot cocoa warms stomachs.

Molly was not out back either. She's probably in the kitchen making sure her dumb old books are safely packed, Jinky decided. If Molly had *those*, and her stamp collection and diary, she wouldn't mind moving to the end of the world.

Jinky kicked at a tuft of grass. If I could pack up the Indians and take them along, I wouldn't mind moving either. But she thought about her folks' whispered conversation and she wasn't sure that even having her team in Nags Head would help.

She ran up the back steps without looking toward the lot where the Indians were probably practicing this minute.

One of the moving men had pushed the stove partway across the inside of the kitchen door. She had to take a deep breath and turn herself thin-wise to squeeze through.

But Molly wasn't in the kitchen. Jinky fished a paper cup from a carton on the sink drain and held it under the faucet without taking off her ball glove.

As she drank, she watched a draft from the open doors stir dust curls where the refrigerator had been. Overhead she heard the hush-hush of her mother's footsteps.

This very night, she thought, we'll be sleeping in that strange house. Will they tell us the real reason for moving as soon as we get there?

Jinky looked around the once so familiar room. The bare windows seemed to stare back at her. Two cardboard boxes packed with books huddled together in the corner like visitors that knew they were not welcome. On top of one box was a calendar still flipped

to June. There was a red circle around the twentieth
—today!

On the wall above the boxes there was a clean oval-
shaped spot where the old-fashioned mirror with the
comb rack had always hung. The mirror used to belong to Grandmother Smith, who had died eleven
years ago in 1945—Jinky could remember the date
because it was the same year she and Molly were born.

The last place their grandmother had lived was Nags
Head, the very same town they were moving to. Could
the secret the folks talked about have something to
do with that?

Jinky walked slowly over to the counter where the
mirror lay now. The little box made to hold combs
and brushes had been emptied of the live plants
Mother usually kept in it.

As Jinky looked down into the cloudy mirror, she
wondered if Father and his own brother, who had
died in the war, used to look at themselves in it when
they were children.

She guessed not with it lying flat like this. Her face
looked funny. She wiggled her nose to be sure it was
really her and not some ghost face out of a long-ago
past staring back from the wavery glass.

She leaned over until her scissor-straight blond
bangs almost touched the mirror and stuck out her
tongue at her own reflection.

Suddenly, from this angle, she saw that the comb
holder wasn't empty after all. Someone had tucked a
little white card inside it.

Jinky pulled the card out. It was sort of important-looking. She gave a low whistle as she read the words:

WHITEHALL DETECTIVE AGENCY
London, England

Edward Scott
Private Detective

Private detective! Jinky gulped. Edward Scott was the man Mother said a lot depended on. Wait till Molly heard about this. How could she keep from telling her now?

Jinky turned the card over. On the back, in Father's neat handwriting, was an address: "Eighty-one King's Highway."

But why, Jinky wondered, would our family need a detective? And why would Mother and Father hire one who lived so far away as England? She bit at a fingernail as she tried to figure it out.

I hate secrets, she thought, especially secrets so important that we have to leave our home and our friends and go off to some strange place that's hanging clear off the edge of the map!

She wished they could put all the furniture back and stay right here in this house. She didn't want to leave Centerville. Pete's sake, she sure didn't want to leave her team, the Indians. And she hated all this secret business about a detective.

Who was the mysterious "she" that Father was whispering about? It was bound to be some person who lived in Nags Head.

Jinky was so deep in her own thoughts that she jumped when she heard footsteps on the bare floor behind her.

MOLLY TELLS ALL

She spun around, but it was only one of the moving men, followed by Molly twirling like a ballerina to show off her stiff nylon underskirts.

Even today, with almost everything packed, Molly had managed to find a ribbon that exactly matched her full yellow skirt. The ribbon held her long hair, as dark as Jinky's was light, in a neat ponytail.

Molly was a little shorter than Jinky, and because of this she made sure everyone understood she was *five* minutes older.

Without looking away from the moving man, who was examining the burners on the stove, Molly said to Jinky, "You'd better put on your dress. And remember, you said I could wear both our new petticoats at one time if I would stay awake till you went to sleep last night."

Jinky glanced at the man to see if he noticed what Molly said. To pay Molly back for blabbing that,

Jinky turned away without answering. Besides, she had no intention of putting on a dress until she pos-i-tive-ly had to.

Still holding the card in her hand, Jinky propped both elbows on the rim of the sink and stared through the window at the crooked pine tree she'd climbed so often that she knew every limb by heart. She listened enviously while Molly began to make friends with the man. It's as easy as catching a high bunt for Molly to talk to grownups, she thought, but at least I know something she doesn't know—yet.

"The house we're moving to," Molly was saying, "is lots bigger than this one. It's like a country *estate*."

The man did not answer, so Molly went on. "We're just renting it, of course. Father is the only one of us who has seen it. It was built by a man named Mr. Mc-Leod. They say he was the wealthiest man in all of North Carolina!"

Jinky heard the workman say, "No fooling?"

"But he only lived in it a few days," Molly added, "and then he died."

Jinky turned and kicked one of the packing boxes. Molly made it seem as if moving to a house where someone had died was something to brag about. Maybe she wouldn't think that was so great if she knew what I know, Jinky thought.

"That's too bad." The workman grunted as he tipped the stove to hoist it onto a squat platform with a ladderlike handle and thick little wheels.

Molly waved her hand. "It happened ages ago. His wife is still alive, though. But of course she hated staying way out in the country alone, so after he died she moved to an apartment right in Nags Head."

"Mmm." The man squared the stove and began strapping it to the handlebar.

The platform rolled a little and Molly brushed her skirts out of the way. "So no one has ever really lived in the house except a caretaker. It already has loads of furniture in it—the house, I mean. Father says we won't even notice our furniture, the house is so big."

Jinky hoped Molly would soon run out of things to say, but no—"The furniture in the house is ver-r-ry old," Molly went on. "Ours is old, too, only this is really old, and valuable. It's genuine Americana!"

The man raised his eyebrows, and Jinky sniffed. When Molly uses big words, she thought, everyone is impressed. When I try it, they laugh. Genuine Americana, phooey. Probably genuine spooky!

"Someday," Molly said, "the house will be a museum, because the widow is going to leave it to the town of Nags Head when she dies."

Jinky threw her ball glove on the counter in disgust. All she can talk about is people dying, she thought. She held the card up and read it again, hoping Molly would notice and ask what it was.

If she does, Jinky thought, and I say, "Oh, it's just a card with the name and address of the detective who works for our family," I'll bet that man would *really* be impressed. And wouldn't Molly be surprised!

But Molly only seemed interested in her own conversation. "Father says our new house has a moat filled with water all the way around it." She gave a little offhand laugh and smoothed her ponytail. "I think it sounds like a castle."

And she thinks she's a *princess*, Jinky thought.

The workman wiped his forehead with the back of his hand. "It sure sounds grand, young lady. You'll be mighty lucky to live in a place like that."

Young *lady*! Jinky wrinkled her nose.

"The only thing is"—Molly hesitated—"there are these two huge dogs living there."

Jinky had almost forgotten about the dogs! At least she had the dogs to look forward to. She hoped the workman could tell how scared Molly was just from thinking about those dogs.

But Jinky was not scared. Pete's sake, Jinky thought, I'm not scared of anything I can *see*. Now ghosts and stuff, that's different. Funny thing about being a twin. Seems like things I'm afraid of are Molly's favorites—like ghosts. And things Molly's afraid of—like dogs—are my favorites.

From the minute Father had said that the caretaker of the house was retiring but the dogs would still live there, Jinky had thought of the dogs as her own. Their names were Duke and Baron.

"One dog is a Doberman and the other a German police." Molly's eyes widened as she explained this to the man. "And Father says you can't get near the place until you've been properly introduced to those dogs. I guess he'll have to introduce us, and you too when you bring our furniture."

Before the man could answer, Molly added, "I like cats much better than dogs. But my twin sister" —she motioned toward Jinky—"likes dogs."

Jinky felt pleased when the man straightened and looked at her for the first time. But all he said was "*Twin* sister? Who'd ever guess it!"

Molly's ponytail swung like a clock pendulum as she glanced at Jinky and back to the man. "Mother says there must have been a mix-up at the hospital when we were born—we're so different."

Jinky rolled her eyes toward the ceiling with an exaggerated sigh to show how silly she thought it was to tell that to a stranger. But Molly didn't seem to notice.

"Well you never can tell," the man said in a serious voice. He tipped the stove. "Many's the time I've read in the newspapers about just such a mix-up." He was still shaking his head when he wheeled the stove out of the kitchen.

Jinky made a face at his back. What a dumb thing for him to say. Pete's sake, he should know Mother was joking. She was sorry now she had bothered to jump no-hands over the rail to impress him.

Molly walked over to the counter where the mirror was lying. Jinky watched her bend over it, exactly as she herself had done. She pictured how Molly's face would look in the dim glass—and suddenly she had to tell Molly about the secret and the card and . . . and . . . But where to begin!

Because Molly had a way of never believing her,

and because the news about the secret *was* hard to believe, Jinky decided to start with the card.

"Look," she said, tossing the card in front of Molly, "this card belongs to a detective who's helping the folks out of some kind of trouble." She watched while Molly read the front of the card then turned it over the same as Jinky herself had done.

"I don't believe you," Molly said at last. "You're always telling fibs."

"Honest," Jinky said. "Cross my heart."

"How do you know?"

"Well, it's a secret and you have to promise you won't tell Mother I told you, but there's a mysterious woman—or girl—where we're going to live who is causing trouble. That's really, truly why we're moving."

"How do you know?" Molly was always so *suspicious*.

"You promised you wouldn't tell now," Jinky reminded her.

"Not yet I didn't," Molly answered.

Too late Jinky realized that she should have made Molly promise before telling her anything at all. She thought fast. "Well, promise, and you can have my new underskirt for the whole summer."

Molly nodded so eagerly it almost made Jinky laugh. She knew that wearing at least two petticoats the way all the girls were doing so their skirts would stand out, gave Molly the same good feeling she herself had when she put on old jeans and a sweatshirt, but she couldn't imagine why. She looked around to make sure no one was coming and then whispered, "I eavesdropped—just a little."

"Hurry and tell me," Molly begged.

"Well"—Jinky tried to make every word sound as exciting as she could—"Father *saw* her. I'm sure he saw her when he went to Nags Head to rent the house. For some reason, when he saw this person he hired a *detective*—that one right there on the card."

Molly looked at the card again. "Hey!" she cried. "This must have come in that letter."

"What letter?"

"The letter from England that I was going to ask for the stamp off of, only Father was sleeping when—"

"But what did the letter say?" Molly could be so maddeningly slow.

"I'm trying to tell you," Molly said, "that when I took his mail up one day Father was asleep, and you know Mother always tells us never to bother him when he's resting—in case it's one of his bad days. So I just left the letter with his other mail."

Jinky could understand this. Though Father never complained, he was in pain a lot of the time. Because of an injury he got fighting for his country in World War II, he had to wear an artificial leg.

Molly cocked her head. "Tell me what else the folks said."

Importantly, Jinky began to tick the facts off on her fingers. "That they needed our help desperately, especially mine, and—"

"Why especially yours?"

Jinky shrugged. "I don't know."

"I'll bet you're lying again, but go on."

"That they weren't going to tell us the secret until Mother saw this mystery person. That a lot depended on the detective, and they needed all the help they could get."

"Hey, I've got it!" Molly's eyes were shining. "It has something to do with Father's new book. Maybe he has located a relative of Virginia Dare. You know she came from England the same as that detective and —hey!" she interrupted herself, "or maybe the 'she' Father was talking about was Virginia Dare's ghost!"

With a quick glance over her shoulder Molly lowered her voice. "In a book I read it said that there is a legend that the ghost of Virginia Dare still roams through the hills around Nags Head. The ghost is invisible, of course, except at the stroke of midnight."

"Phooey," Jinky said uneasily, "I don't believe it. Besides, who'd hire a detective to chase a ghost?"

"Someone might," Molly said, "if they were writing a book about the person whose ghost it was and had a clue that needed to be investigated. Yes"—she nodded —"I'm sure that's it. Won't it be exciting? Maybe Father and the detective will take us on the ghost hunt with them."

"I don't think the 'she' was a ghost at all," Jinky argued. She didn't even like to think about that Virginia Dare ghost business. "After all, I was the one who heard them talking."

"You hope it wasn't a ghost. You're scared of ghosts."

"I am not!" Jinky said fiercely. But she was. A mysterious person was sort of exciting, but a ghost—one that walked at midnight!

Molly looked smug. "You try to *pretend* you don't believe in ghosts and I know why. I'll *ask* Father about that card, if you'll let me have both petticoats anyway."

"No! Don't ask him," Jinky yelled—then clapped her hand over her mouth because Mother came rushing through the kitchen doorway.

Jinky barely managed to slip the card back into the old mirror before Mother turned to her and began scolding because she wasn't dressed for the trip. "Your dress is laid out. I couldn't *find* your good petticoat. And come right back down, because I want you both to help carry things to the car."

But even in the flurry of actually starting out for their new home, Jinky couldn't forget the mysterious "she," *nor* the secret which it was more important for her to help with than Molly, *nor* the detective.

She buried them deep in her mind the way a dog buries a bone, planning to dig them up and worry over them later.

JOURNEY INTO SHADOWS

Everyone was loaded into the car at last. Mother said she'd be glad to drive all the way, and Jinky knew this was to keep Father from getting too tired.

Jinky and Molly were crowded into the back seat along with pillows, the picnic basket, a china lamp too fragile to trust to the movers, Jinky's ball glove, and a stack of Molly's books.

As Jinky settled back on the seat, she banged her elbow against something hard. It was Grandmother Smith's mirror. Since Mother always called this her only "honest antique," she must have decided she couldn't trust it to the moving van either. Or was it in the car because of the card inside it?

Jinky watched Molly pick up a book and begin to read. Molly has probably forgotten the detective already, she thought. Ghost hunt, ha! It would serve Molly right if I solved this mystery by myself.

Cautiously Jinky slid her fingers along the rusty

lining of the comb holder until she touched the detective's card. It was her best clue so far.

While she watched from the corner of her eye to be sure Molly stayed deep in *The Secret Garden,* Jinky sneaked the card out of the tray.

She pretended to be interested in the scenery as she leaned forward, pulled off her sneaker, and slipped the card inside it.

When she had scrunched her foot back into her shoe, she tried once more to figure out why Father would need a detective's help. Was the detective going to come all the way from England?

Maybe, Jinky thought with a little shudder, maybe Molly is right. She usually is. Maybe the mysterious "she" is a ghost. That would mean Father had *seen* a ghost! And when Mother had said she had to be careful about explaining how they needed Jinky's help, had she meant because Jinky was afraid of ghosts?

Jinky wished she could forget the whole thing. She tried to concentrate on the pine trees flashing past the open car window. The shorter, younger trees were topped with light green needles which looked like birthday candles.

At last Molly stretched, yawned, then as if suddenly dropping back from the silent world of words to the real world, she snapped her book shut. She put it neatly with the others and perched on the edge of the seat. "I'm so glad we're moving," she said.

Listening, Jinky thought once again how strange it was to be a twin. I know exactly how Molly feels, she admitted to herself, but the same thing that makes Molly all bubbly and glad inside makes me feel like I got whomped in the stomach with a hard-pitched ball.

"I hope," Molly went on, "that we get to our new house while it's still light enough to explore."

Father pulled a map from the glove compartment. "I imagine it will be dark when we get there," he answered Molly. "But there's always tomorrow." His mouth smiled but his eyes didn't. "Before it gets dark," he said, "you'll see signs marking the Virginia Dare Trail Highway. That takes us right into Nags Head."

Though Father seemed to be studying the map, Jinky wondered if his thoughts were really on the secret he and Mother—

"Just think!" Molly interrupted Jinky's thoughts, "we'll be living in the same place Virginia Dare was born—maybe even on the very spot where she disappeared! Have you already started investigating about her for your book?"

Jinky jabbed Molly with her elbow to remind her of the promise. She felt relieved when Molly said, "I mean, I hope this book will be a mystery, a sort of history-mystery, like the one you wrote about Aaron Burr's beautiful daughter, Theodosia. I liked the part best where she was captured by the pirates when she was on her way to find her father. That's my favorite book in the whole world."

Jinky saw a little stain of pleasure color Father's

JOURNEY INTO SHADOWS   31

thin cheeks as he answered, "Yes, this will be another fictionalized biography—the story of Virginia Dare. I don't have many facts to go on, but the story will be based on what few facts were recorded. Glad you liked *Young Theodosia*, Molly."

Jinky could have hugged Molly for making Father look so happy, and she wished desperately that she had read his book, too.

Every now and then, she thought, it almost seems as if Molly and I are the same person, instead of being twins—one person, with a good and a bad side. And I'm the bad side, she admitted, kind of enjoying the idea.

At that moment the feeling of "twinness" was so strong that, without even knowing it was going to happen, Jinky heard her own voice saying, "It really was *my* favorite book!"

As soon as she said it, Jinky knew it was a mistake.

"You haven't even read *Young Theodosia*," Molly cried, exploding the nice warm feeling that had been there a second ago. "You never read books!"

Jinky stole a quick look at Father, then faced Molly. "That's what you think!"

Molly's eyes widened. "That's what I *know*."

"You *think* you know everything."

"Well have you or haven't you read the book, Jinky?" Mother asked quietly without taking her eyes off the road ahead.

Jinky felt pinned down like a bug under a microscope while everyone waited for her answer. She could feel herself getting madder and madder, the way she did when someone called a ball foul and she thought it was fair. "You don't have to read a book to know if it's your favorite one or not," she yelled.

And then, without warning, it was as if the ball had been declared fair after all, as if she were running free and fast toward first base, because Father smiled, even with his eyes, and said, "That's right, Jinky, you don't—if you have enough confidence in its author."

A sudden cooling breeze came through the car windows, and to Jinky it seemed to blow away the anger along with the heat. She leaned toward Molly and whispered, "I'm sorry."

"That's okay," Molly said.

Jinky felt even better—kind of cozy—as she saw the pleased look that passed between her parents. It was a look which Jinky secretly called their "clothesline look." Her parents' clothesline look seemed to be hung with all sorts of little personal thoughts and understandings, and though it always passed straight between Mother and Father, invisible magic loops of it included Molly and Jinky, too.

Jinky propped up her feet on the back of the front seat, closed her eyes, and made herself a vow: When I solve the mystery about why we're moving to Nags Head, and get used to that house, I'm going to try to be more like Molly. In her mind she named over the things this would mean.

Read all Father's books.
Always tell the exact truth.
Quit eavesdropping.
Think of interesting things to say to grownups.

Wear dresses more of the time.
Stop chewing off fingernails.
Not play baseball with boys, even if I get a chance.

As Jinky tried to decide whether or not to cross off that last promise, she heard Father say, "That shady spot ahead looks like a good place to stop for our picnic lunch."

When lunch was finished and they were getting back into the car, Jinky noticed that Father was leaning on his cane more heavily than usual. He sighed as he slid into the front seat.

"You worked too hard on the packing up," Mother said, taking the seat behind the wheel.

"I *am* having a little trouble with this hip," Father admitted.

Little trouble, Jinky thought, loving Father very much because he was always so brave. As if having an artificial leg was nothing! If he'd had better care when he was wounded, instead of being locked up in a prisoner of war camp, he wouldn't have so much pain.

Jinky looked out the window. The shadows were getting longer. The car moved more slowly as they wound into hills thickly needled with slender pines.

She dozed, and when she awoke, the thick groves of loblolly and shortleaf pines had begun to thin. Before long they crossed the Wright Memorial Bridge, and Molly explained that it was named after Wilbur and Orville Wright, who built the first successful airplane.

"I already know that," Jinky said, feeling mixed

up and cross after her nap. Then she remembered her vow to always tell the exact truth and added, "At least I *heard* about Wilbur Wright once."

Now, along the roadside, instead of the red clay soil they were used to seeing, there was white sand. In some places it was piled up into high wind-smoothed dunes.

Like giant slices of cake with sea oat for trim on the icing, Jinky thought.

The world turned a greenish mixture of lightness and darkness, and from the car window Jinky saw miles of rolling beachland and flat meadows. The cool damp air smelled sharp as salt.

"Are we almost there?" Molly asked from her corner.

"Almost," Father answered, and Jinky thought his voice sounded tired. Or now that they were so near Nags Head, was he worried about the secret reason for coming here? Jinky wiggled her toes against the card she had hidden in her sneaker and vowed to help just as quickly as she could.

Then all at once Father was saying, "Just ahead, where the hedgerow begins—the private drive."

Mother braked and turned off onto a road that was barely as wide as the car itself. The sandy-looking path cut through a field of broomsedge grasses and tall weeds.

In the near dark it seemed to Jinky as if they had dropped into a sea of blurred reds and yellows, as if this car were the only moving thing in the whole world.

And then, with a little gasp, she pointed out her window to a patch of moving weeds. "What's that?"

A shadowy form raced through the high grass beside the road. Swiftly, silently it kept pace with their car.

"There's something on this side, too," Molly said in a voice no louder than half a whisper.

THE GHOST OF VIRGINIA DARE

Jinky grabbed for the handle to roll her window up as Father said, "It's only the dogs, Duke and Baron." His voice was sharp and edgy. "Don't you remember? I told you they escort every car that comes down this drive."

Whew! Jinky felt so silly she couldn't keep from grinning. Molly didn't smile though. She pressed her lips together and looked mad as mud. When Molly was scared, which was seldom, or when she was wrong about something, which was hardly ever, she usually hid her *real* feelings behind crossness.

Jinky decided that probably Father was hiding behind crossness, too, trying to keep everyone from knowing he was plain worn out, and maybe even hurting from the hours of riding. I'm the one who should have remembered about the dogs, Jinky thought. After all, for me at least, they're the one good thing about moving here.

She tried to get a look at the dog on her side of the car, but he was still only a streaking shadow. She searched the path of their headlights, half dreading to see the house and half wanting to get it over with.

Now she saw that they were coming to a narrow bridge. It was flat, without railings, and she decided it must be the place to cross the moat. There were thick bushes spreading out from the bridge in both directions.

As Mother eased their car onto the bridge, Father, sounding as if he were sorry for being cross and wanting to make up for it, explained that the moat was actually a swift creek that overlapped itself in places, like a coil of garden hose. "Those hollylike bushes along the banks are yaupon," he told them. "That's why Mrs. McLeod named this the Yaupon Moat house."

Just as he said the name of the house, Jinky saw it looming ahead. Big as it was, it was half hidden in the deep shadows of huge live oaks. The words "shrouded by mist" popped into Jinky's mind, and she wished she had the courage to say them out loud. They were exactly the kind of words Molly used all the time.

The road ended in a circle drive. Mother shut off the motor and an enormous silence, big as the night, settled over everything as all four of them dipped their heads to look toward the house.

Set back in the stillness, with the night mist drifting in and out of its pillared porches, the house seemed to be breathing—and waiting.

Outside the car the dogs were waiting, too.

"Well, we're here at last," Father said. Then he turned to Molly. "You'll see how well-trained Duke and Baron are. They'll remember having been introduced to me before."

"I hope so," Molly said, some of the crossness still in her voice.

To show Father that she certainly was not afraid of those dogs, Pete's sake, Jinky squeezed past the boxes and suitcases and jumped out ahead of Molly.

The dogs did seem to remember Father, because they didn't bark. They sat like iron statues, barely panting after the race with the car. Duke was a handsome brown German police, and Baron, the Doberman, was as black and shiny as water in a night puddle.

While a frog somewhere back in the yard croaked as if it disapproved of this interruption, Father called to both dogs and introduced them to his family.

"And this is Jinky," Father finished in as polite a voice as if the dogs were people. Duke got up and rubbed his sleek side against Jinky's droopy skirt. "He likes me already," Jinky said, feeling especially proud, since Molly was almost *behind* Father.

Jinky took the suitcase Mother gave her and put her other hand on Duke's head. The dog moved along beside her as all of them followed Father toward the house.

There was no moon, but the windows on the front of the house glowed as if the moon were stuck somewhere inside it.

The big trees dripped patterns that looked like
black witch's lace over the yard. Jinky lagged behind
the others long enough to get a better look at the
house before they went inside. As she looked up, she
saw that one of two little windows under the top gable
had been boarded up. It made that part of the house
look like a pirate's face with a patch over one eye.
Jinky's toes curled inside her sneakers. Did someone
break that window trying to get in—or out?

She was about to hurry and catch up, but suddenly
she stopped. *Something was standing in the shadows
of that tree!* She dropped her suitcase and ran around
to the other side of Duke so he was between her and
the—thing.

Did "it" move, or was that only a breeze stirring
the leaves above "its" head? Jinky would have run to
the others, but her feet seemed to belong to somebody
else, somebody stupid enough to just stand there and
look, Pete's sake!

Now her eyes were getting used to the dark. She
stared at what surely must be—a girl!

The prickly feeling that had started on Jinky's
back spread all over her. That was—that had to be—
a girl, standing stock-still, not ten feet away, watching
Jinky from her hiding place under that tree.

Why didn't Duke bark? Was the girl someone he
was used to seeing around here, someone who lived
close enough to come often? But there had been no
houses back this far along the drive from the main
road.

Jinky almost jumped out of her skin when Mother's voice came cutting across her scaredness. "Come along, Jinky, the door's unlocked now."

Jinky reached cautiously for her suitcase. "L-let's go, Duke," she said, more to let her feet know they *could* move than to command the dog. Without daring to glance back, she sprinted across the rest of the stepping stones hit or miss until she reached her family.

"There's a—" Jinky gasped, but stopped. What if that silent shadowlike figure had been nothing but a strange kind of bush? Or maybe it had been only her imagination.

If they looked, and nobody was there, they'd laugh and call her a worry-wart. It would spoil her not being afraid of the dogs when Molly was.

Anyway, everyone seemed so eager to see the inside of the house that they hadn't heard what she started to say.

And then, crowded safely between Mother and Father, but careful not to joggle against Father, Jinky was glad she hadn't told them, because *maybe* this was her next clue. *Maybe* that girl was the mysterious "she" Father had seen. Tomorrow in broad daylight she'd hunt for footprints under that tree.

But Jinky's stomach still felt like the highest dip on a roller coaster as she went into the wide entryway with her family. The hall was empty except for a coat tree with hooks that looked like curled fingers.

Even without lights it didn't seem completely dark in the house. Jinky realized that the strange glow she'd seen in the windows from outside was coming from the living room.

Pete's sake, that glow was nothing but little hooded lights someone had left burning above two big pictures on the living-room wall. Probably, Jinky promised herself, there is just as ordinary a reason for that girl to be standing out there alone in the night, too. But she shivered anyway.

Father flipped a switch, and lamps all around the huge high-ceilinged room sprang to life, throwing shadow lamps above them on the white walls. "How do you like it?" Father asked Mother.

Jinky didn't hear Mother's answer. She was busy staring in astonishment at what must be the biggest fireplace in the whole world.

Beside the fireplace were three spinning wheels. One was big, one middle-sized, and one small. Like the three bears' house, Jinky thought, feeling as out of place as Goldilocks.

She looked around at the stiff sofas with high backs, at the puffy-chested red platform rocker, and at all those old-fashioned lamps with chimneys. How could *this* ever seem like home?

Jinky wondered how Molly felt about this house now that they were here. Did it still seem like a castle to her? Jinky couldn't tell by the expression on her sister's face.

Slowly, the way people move when they're feeling their way in the dark, they all went into the big dining room.

"A harvest table." Mother ran her fingertips along

its plain oak surface. On both sides of the narrow table were heavy carved chairs. "It's . . . lovely," Mother added. But Jinky heard her voice catch on a little snag of doubt.

Father must have heard it, too, because he said extra cheerfully, "And real deacon's benches!" He motioned to the two stiff benches backed against one wall like they were waiting for their turn at the table.

Again Jinky looked around the long shadowy room. She felt as if she and all her family had shrunk to tiny doll figures, as if a giant hand were moving them about and a ventriloquist saying their words.

Jinky tried, by setting her heels down before her toes, to keep from tiptoeing as they went into the big white kitchen. Then she followed along as they went back through the dining room and living room to climb the sweeping curve of stairs.

Upstairs, behind so many doors that Jinky lost count, were poster beds, marble-topped dressers, and washstands with pitchers and basins used before people had sinks.

Just outside one room, toward the back of the house, there was a funny old clock that Mother said was a wag-on-the-wall. The clock had wooden workings with no box to cover them.

Inside the room were two beds, smaller than the ones in the other rooms. These beds had dainty flowered canopies over the tops of them and two short ladders beside them. There was a little rocking chair that Mother called a banister-back, and on the top knob of the chair was fastened a petticoat lamp.

Of course Molly fell in love with the frilly little lamp as soon as she learned its name, and Mother said that the twins might share this room.

"There's nothing on the third floor but the attic," Father said, and Jinky's thoughts flew to the boarded window. She vowed never to go up there, not even in broad daylight.

Mother said she and Father would take the room just across the hall, and Jinky was glad of that.

Before long Jinky and Molly were in their night-gowns and huddled under mounds of scallop-edged quilts.

"Do you suppose people in the town will think we're rich?" Molly asked. "I mean, living in such an elegant house as this."

"They might," Jinky answered, because she knew that was what Molly wanted her to say. Secretly though, she didn't think they would, because Father had said the only reason they could afford this house was that its owner needed them to replace the old caretaker, and that the owner was more interested in someone to take care of it than in getting much money. "Do you like this house, Molly?"

"Yes," Molly said in a voice so wobbly that Jinky knew that for once Molly couldn't make up her mind. But Molly sounded more like her old self as she added, "I just know I'll like it when it's daytime and we can explore. I already feel like I'm living between the pages of a book."

"Well, close the book and go to sleep," Mother

said unexpectedly from the doorway. "Your father's very tired. It's been a long day."

Though they said they would, and blew sleep-tight kisses as they always had done from their big bed back home, Jinky herself had no intention of letting Molly go to sleep first. She had already promised away her new petticoat and she couldn't think of anything else Molly would want, so she decided that every time Molly started to go to sleep she would talk.

Sure enough, Mother had no sooner opened the long window behind their beds and turned off the little lamp than Molly yawned peacefully.

The boards of the big house creaked just above Jinky's canopy and she scooted deeper into the covers, trying to think of something to say interesting enough to keep Molly awake. Pete's sake, if Molly had seen what she saw tonight under that tree she'd be so— "Molly!" Jinky whispered. "Wake up if you're asleep. I've got something to tell you."

"I'm listening," Molly said drowsily.

"You've got to believe me," Jinky said and began telling about the shadowy figure under the big oak out front. She did not exaggerate one word and even admitted that Duke had seen "it," but hadn't barked. "So don't you see," she finished, "it was probably somebody Duke knows. But what was she doing out there in the dark?"

Jinky had expected her story to keep Molly awake —*if* she believed it. But she never dreamed Molly would act the way she did.

Molly sat straight up in bed and whispered, "You saw it!"

"Saw what, Pete's sake?"

"The ghost of Virginia Dare!"

UNEXPECTED COMPANY

"You *saw* the ghost of Virginia Dare," Molly repeated. "I told you that I read there was one around Nags Head. This house is exactly the sort of place a ghost would like. That's why Duke didn't bark; dogs can't see ghosts. Don't you see? The dog not barking proves it."

Jinky pulled her covers up to her eyes. She reminded herself that Molly always believed everything she read in books. This didn't help much, though, when Jinky thought about how ghostlike that figure under the tree had been.

But that couldn't have been a ghost, she told herself sternly, because there isn't such a thing. She inched her covers down just long enough to say, "Phooey!" then tightened them back around her ears.

"If you knew what I know," Molly insisted, "you'd believe in Virginia Dare's ghost."

"Okay, what?" This was a terrible time to listen to a ghost story, but at least Molly would have to stay awake to tell it.

Molly rolled her pillow and propped herself facing Jinky. "A long time ago a little group of people came to the American colonies from England and settled right here where Nags Head is today. Remember I told you they were the first white people to live in America, and one of the women had a baby named Virginia Dare. Their leader was Governor White, who was also Virginia Dare's grandfather.

"Governor White had to go back to England to get more supplies. He was gone a long time because England was fighting the Spanish Armada and he couldn't start back when he wanted to. By the time the seas were safe and he came back, the little colony had disappeared; Virginia Dare, too, very mysteriously."

Jinky was curled on her side watching Molly's face in the dim light from the hall. Her eyes began to feel heavy, and she let them slide closed and murmured, "I don't see anything so ghostly about that."

"You will," Molly promised. "Just wait until I get to the Indian-legend part. The people around here really believe it, so I do, too, because they should know. Jinky, do you even know what a legend is?"

Jinky opened her eyes. "I'm not as dumb as you think!"

"All right, what is a legend?"

"It's a . . . s-story. That's all."

Molly traced one finger slowly around a quilt scallop. "It's a whole lot more than that, Jinky. Now don't get huffy again. I don't get mad because you're a good baseball player and I'm not."

"That's different."

Molly shrugged. "Anyway, it helps if you know that a legend is something someone *saw* happen. The thing they saw was so important they told their children, who remembered it and told it to their children, and they told theirs, and so on, until it gets to be a legend."

"Somebody might have fibbed," Jinky said.

"Jinky, I *read* this legend. Besides that, Indians were very honest people. I figure this legend is as true as history—practically."

Jinky yawned. Molly was beginning to sound so much like a schoolteacher that she was making her sleepy, and that suited Jinky just fine.

"Now listen." Molly's voice grew suddenly low and mysterious, so that Jinky had a hard time keeping her eyes closed. "The legend, which most people believe, is that an Indian tribe stole the baby Virginia Dare and adopted her for their own. She grew to be a beautiful maiden, and she and a young Indian brave named Okisco fell in love.

"But," Molly went on, "a magician in that tribe, named Chico, loved Virginia Dare, too."

Jinky pictured Virginia Dare dressed like an Indian maid, except she would be pale and have long golden hair. "Go on," she whispered.

"The magician, Chico, wanted to keep the Indian

brave from having Virginia Dare, so he changed Virginia into a white doe."

"Phooey," Jinky said, completely awake now. "I don't believe it."

"Then maybe you don't want to hear the rest."

"Go on."

"Well, there was another magician. He was from a different tribe. He gave the Indian brave, Okisco, a silver arrow that would magically turn Virginia Dare into a maiden again if it pierced the white doe's heart."

"This is sure hard to believe."

"Jinky!"

"Okay."

"When the Indian brave shot the doe through the heart"—Molly paused and took a deep breath—"a mist rose up, and there lay Virginia Dare—dead!"

"Dead?" Jinky caught herself repeating. "But that magician—*Clear* dead?"

"Yes," Molly whispered. "And ever since, even to this very day, her ghost roams through the hills around Nags Head, visible only at the stroke of midnight."

Jinky turned her head slowly and looked at the open window. Thoughts of the form standing in the shadows along the path returned to haunt her mind. But then she remembered something. "If that was Virginia Dare's ghost I saw, how come it was visible *before* midnight?"

Molly sighed. "I give up," she said and turned her back.

"Ha! You can't answer that," Jinky said, feeling pleased with herself.

"I could, but I won't," Molly answered crossly, and Jinky knew what that meant, all right. It always made Molly cross to be wrong and she *had* said the ghost appeared only at midnight.

Jinky lay as still as she could in the strange narrow bed. In spite of the feather mattress, she felt as if a cold finger were tracing down her spine.

Molly began to breathe deeper and deeper, and at the same time the wag-on-the-wall clock outside the door seemed to be ticking louder and louder.

In the splinter of light from the hall Jinky could barely see the clock's flower-painted face with two little figures dancing inside a circle over the twelve. How long was it until the stroke of midnight?

Jinky lay there watching the outline of the pendulum wagging back and forth like a gossipy tongue. It seemed to say, "Stroke-of-twelve, tock-tock-tock. Stroke-of-twelve, tock-tock-tock."

The suspense got to be more than Jinky could bear. Slowly she pushed her covers back and crept over to the door to see what time the wag-on-the-wall said.

Pete's sake! Only five after ten. From here Jinky could hear the comforting murmur of her parents' voices across the hall. She thought again of the secret they had discussed in their bedroom back home. Did that happen only this morning? It seemed like a million years ago.

Jinky started back to bed. From the open window

she could hear a whole chorus of frogs croaking, "Ribbit, ribbit, ribbit," and the gurgling of the water in the moat, like a giant drinking out of a huge dipper, and then suddenly she heard a new sound.

There was a car coming down the drive toward the house.

The car's motor chugged to a stop. For a second there was no sound except the night noises again, and then the dogs, Duke and Baron, began to bark wildly.

Whoever is out there, Jinky thought, has certainly not been introduced to the dogs!

DROWNING CREEK

Jinky heard footsteps in the hall outside her door. She peeked out and saw that both Mother and Father were going to investigate the commotion.

And that Molly! She was sleeping soundly through the whole thing. Jinky reminded herself that ghosts don't drive cars, and dogs don't bark at ghosts anyway. As soon as she was sure her parents were downstairs, she crept silently along the hallway. She hunched herself on the top step as wild plans whizzed through her mind of what she would do if her folks were in danger.

She heard the heavy front door whoosh open and Father shout, "Who's there?" Father isn't afraid, she thought proudly. She guessed that after fighting in a war and almost dying in that prison camp nothing could scare him.

She caught her breath as a man's voice drawled, "I'll tell you as soon as you quiet these dratted dogs."

"Duke! Baron! It's all right," Father called, and the barking stopped.

Jinky slid down one step. Father was letting the stranger in. Or maybe he was not a stranger to Father. Maybe he was that detective, Edward Scott. But no—

"I'm Emmet Saunders," the slow voice said, "and I got a wireless for you-all. That is, I have if you're James Smith."

"I am," Father said, "and this is Mrs. Smith."

"I reckoned you must be the Smiths, otherwise what would you be doing out here in this house on Drownin' Creek?"

"Drowning Creek?" Father questioned. "Mrs. Mc-Leod calls it Yaupon Moat."

"It's all right with me," the man replied, "if it pleasures you comers 'n' goers to pretty up Drownin' Creek and call it Yaupon Moat. But Drownin' Creek is what it always was to us Bankers, and so Drownin' Creek it's gonna stay."

Banker? Jinky scooted down two more steps to get a better look at the man. He didn't look like a banker —wearing overalls. Though he was thin like Father, his face was seamy as the hide of a baseball. He held a yellow envelope between one finger and his thumb as if he thought bad news inside it might rub off on him.

Who could be sending the Smiths a telegram?

Seeming to read Jinky's mind, Emmet Saunders said, "This ain't no regular telegram. It came all the way from England."

The detective! Shivering with excitement, Jinky tucked her nightgown around her toes. She hugged her knees. Maybe she would learn the folks' secret! She wished that funny banker man would hurry and give the telegram to Father.

But now that he'd come all the way out here, in the middle of the night practically, Emmet Saunders seemed in no rush. "This place is sure filled with pretties," he said, looking around curiously. "First time I been inside it. Not many of us Bankers have. Ain't been invited."

Pete's sake, he sure doesn't talk like a banker, either, Jinky thought.

"Look around all you like," Father said as Emmet Saunders strolled across the room.

Whoops! He was coming toward the stairs. Jinky barely had time to scramble from sight as Emmet Saunders headed toward the kitchen door. "Course I wasn't no friend of Mr. McLeod's myself," he said over his shoulder, "but I recollect him. Mighty personable man." He pushed the kitchen door open a crack, peeked in, then let it swing shut and added, "Shame he never got a chance to enjoy this house before he was murdered."

"Murdered!"

Jinky almost tumbled down the steps. For a scary second she thought it had been her own voice echoing that awful word, giving away her hiding place.

But then she realized it was Mother who had said it, because Emmet Saunders looked at Mother and answered, "You could say he was, ma'am, or again you could say he wasn't. Now don't get the idea folks don't like his widow woman. She's no Banker, but though she lives Ocean Side, I have to admire that she isn't exactly a comer 'n' goer, either. And she did give the money to build our orphanage."

That poor Mrs. McLeod! Jinky thought. No wonder she hated living alone in this house—if her husband was murdered here. Did it really happen right here in this very house? Jinky began to get a creepy feeling, as if someone were staring at her back. Slowly she looked over one shoulder, then the other. But there was no one in the hall, and only witching shadows in the darkened bedrooms beyond.

Jinky had a strong urge to fly down the stairs and snuggle up close to someone. Even if they scolded because she was still awake, it would be better than sitting up here alone.

But if I go down, she thought, squaring her shoulders, Mother will just send me back to bed and I won't get to hear the telegram. If the folks *are* in some kind of trouble, I might be able to help them like Mother said. But I can't help unless I know what the trouble is.

Just then, in the room below, Emmet Saunders yawned and held the yellow envelope out to Father. "Guess I'd better get on back to town," he said. "So if you'll just speak to those dogs again . . ."

Now! Jinky thought when she heard the door being locked behind the visitor. She slid back down two steps.

Even before Emmet Saunders' car started up, Father ripped open the envelope. But, Pete's sake, he was holding the message so that he and Mother could read it at the same time—to themselves!

"That's what you get," Jinky's conscience scolded, "for eavesdropping."

Jinky ignored her conscience and searched her parents' faces to see if the telegram was bad news or not. She decided that their faces had a kind of let-down look.

At last Mother spoke, but so softly that Jinky had to strain to hear. "Everything is up to us from here on. You know, Jim, now that I'm going to see her for myself, I'm almost afraid."

Father put his arm across Mother's shoulder. "I know how you feel. But we'll see this through together. I can tell you this much. When you see her, you're in for a shock."

Shock? Jinky propped her elbows on her knees and dug her fists into her cheeks. She watched Mother walk over to the window and pull back the drapery. "To think," Mother said over her shoulder, "that she's out there somewhere right now—so close."

Out there right now? Jinky thought again of the figure she had seen in the shadows, the figure Molly said was the ghost of Virginia Dare. What—? But suddenly Jinky's scary thoughts were interrupted by a clatter from below.

She looked quickly toward Father and saw that the clatter had been his cane falling to the wide floorboards as he slumped down onto the sofa.

Mother ran toward him. "Jim! What's the matter?"

"Nothing, nothing at all," Father said almost angrily. "Just a little tired."

"Let's get you to bed this very . . ."

Jinky dared wait no longer. She streaked for her own bedroom, fighting back tears of worry and misery all the way—worry about Father, and the way everything seemed so mixed up.

Was Father this upset because the mysterious "she" really was the ghost of Virginia Dare? Was that why Mother said she was afraid to see her? And was that why Father said Mother was going to be shocked when she did?

Jinky raced into her bedroom and shook her sister's shoulder. "Molly, wake up!" she whispered desperately.

Molly rubbed her eyes. "Huh? What?"

"Shh," Jinky warned, "the folks will hear you. Someone came out here with a telegram for Father."

"You've been dreaming." Molly sighed. "It's the middle of the night. Go back to sleep."

Jinky heard her parents coming slowly up the stairs. There was no time to lose. "Honest," she pleaded. "Please believe me. It was about that mysterious 'she'!"

"M-m." Molly snuggled deeper into her pillow and muttered, "You're making all this up to keep me awake."

"I'm *not*. Do you know what happened to the man who built this house? He was *murdered*. Maybe in this very room!"

"Fibber." Molly yawned and turned her face away. Almost at once she began to breathe heavily again.

Now Jinky could tell that the folks were in the hall and headed this way. Oh, why couldn't Molly believe her just one time! She hopped into bed and stuck out her tongue at Molly's back. "I wouldn't be like *you* for a million dollars," she whispered, keeping a cautious eye on the doorway. "Bookworm!"

Jinky flopped to her back and stared up into the canopy until its design became a quivering blur through her tears. At last she rolled over and looked toward the window. Ghostly wisps of fog blew across the screen, and she thought of Mother staring into the night and saying, "She's out there somewhere right now—so close."

Was it midnight yet?

Jinky squeezed her eyes tight and lay very stiff and still, listening to the eerie gurgling of Drowning Creek, or Yaupon Moat, or whatever it really was. Moving day seemed . . . to . . . be . . . going to last forev . . .

THE GIRL UNDER THE TREE

The next thing Jinky knew it was daylight. For a second she wondered where she was. Then she remembered, and her next thought was about Father. Was he feeling better this morning? And what about the telegram?

She saw that Molly's bed was not only empty but also made up as neat as Molly herself. Jinky hopped up, feeling cheated because she had overslept, and began rummaging helter-skelter through her old brown suitcase for her jeans and a sweatshirt.

As soon as she found them, she buried yesterday's pile of clothes under the folded ones and, yanking on the sweatshirt over her head, dashed to look out the window.

The thick limbs of the gnarled trees below were hung with long tangles of gray moss like the hair of a thousand witches scalped in the night. What would she find this morning under that big tree?

60

Jinky could see mist still drifting along the ground, but instead of gray night mist, this was a more friendly-looking morning mist—pale yellow. Father said on the way here that the sun came up out of the ocean and set in the Sound, so according to where the sun was now, the Sound would be to the back of the house. What a strange, quiet world this was out here on this long tail of land that was almost an island.

Where is everybody? Jinky wondered as she ran to the dresser and grabbed up Molly's brush. She gave her hair a hurried smoothing so Mother wouldn't send her straight back to her room.

There was so much to see and so much to find out today. Maybe, now that the telegram had come, the folks would be ready to tell the secret.

Through the mirror Jinky noticed that Molly had unpacked her good white dress and spread it on the little rocker. The dress sort of matched the prissy petticoat lamp, and both of them matched Molly.

That Molly better not have gone outdoors without me, Jinky thought.

Just then Molly popped through the doorway. Her ponytail was tied with a green bow to match her second-best dress, and she was bustling with importance—and *both* petticoats.

"You're to come down and eat now," Molly told her. "Father hurt himself lifting too many things yesterday, and he has to stay in bed until the moving van brings his crutches. Mother says it isn't serious, but she's going to call a doctor."

So Father was really sick! Calling the doctor sounded awfully serious to Jinky.

Molly put both hands around a footpost of her bed and swung herself back and forth. "While you were still asleep, Mother and I went to town, to Nags Head, and bought a lot of groceries. So I've already seen the ocean—it's wonderful—and the town, *and* the highest sand dune in the world, which is named Jocky Ridge." Molly stopped swinging and faced Jinky. "And you're in trouble because you snooped about the telegram last night."

Jinky blinked as if a fast curve had just whizzed past her ball bat. She let the brush fall. There was only one way the folks could have found out that she had eavesdropped last night. She picked up the brush and pointed it at Molly. "You told!"

"I had to see if you were telling the truth when you woke me up in the night."

Jinky narrowed her eyes until Molly's face was a crisscross of tiny eyelash lines. "What did Mother say?"

"She asked me how much you knew, about the telegram and everything."

Jinky pushed her face up close to Molly's. "And what did you tell her?"

"All I said was that you thought they were going to tell us something about somebody important that Father had seen when he—"

"*Take off my petticoat!*"

"I will not!"

"You broke your promise."

"I did not!" Molly put her hands on her hips, stuck her nose in the air, and said, "I only answered what I was asked, and that's called *honesty* in case you didn't know. I guess everyone in this whole family knows that *you* don't know what honesty is. Even Father doesn't believe half the things you say."

Jinky fought back stinging tears. Now Father knew she had eavesdropped again. And he was sick . . . and . . . "I hope you're satisfied, *snitcher*," she whispered, glancing at the same time toward Father's bedroom.

"I might as well tell you," Molly said, her expression prim as a new-sharpened pencil, "the telegram *was* about the secret, and they *were* going to tell us what it was today. But Mother's too upset about Father to do it now. And anyway she says it's too important to tell until she has plenty of time. She says maybe later this afternoon."

Some of Jinky's anger drained away as she watched Molly's face grow pink with excitement. "I just know," Molly continued, "the telegram has something to do with Father's new book. After all, it's a story about Virginia Dare, whose mother and father came from England the same as that detective.

"I think," Molly went on, "that Father has discovered something very important about Virginia Dare—maybe it will even make him famous. And since that was the reason we moved here, where her ghost still walks at night, it must be something about her ghost."

Jinky already had her mouth open to admit Molly

must be right because of what Mother had said last night about "her" being out there somewhere, when Molly said, "Oh, and besides all that, I saw *your* girl under the tree." Molly gulped as if she were trying to swallow a big laugh. "She's still there if you care to look. I was right in a way"—Molly giggled— "your girl really is Virginia Dare." With that, Molly ran from the room.

Jinky felt like yelling after her, "I hate you!" She would have, too, if she hadn't been afraid Father would hear. What did Molly mean when she said the girl was still standing there? Why did Molly always seem to know everything, to be always right?

Well, she had to go find out, but no matter what she discovered under that tree, she was never ever going to tell Molly Smith another thing as long as she lived.

As Jinky dashed down the hall, she felt the detective's card in the bottom of her sneaker. She'd forgotten about putting it there. She'd forgotten to tie her laces, too, and they made little clicks as she sprinted down the bare steps.

Outside, Jinky could almost *feel* the ocean. A strong wind had sprung up since she'd looked out the window, sweeping away the last bit of mist. The salt sea wind tossed the hanging moss and leaves above Jinky's head, making her feel reckless as she ran down the stepping-stone path.

But when she was almost to the biggest oak, her knees felt spongy with suspense and she slowed down. Molly had said the girl was still there!

Jinky reached the tree and stopped short, catching her breath. The girl *was* there, just as Molly had said. But she was only a statue!

Jinky's shoulders dropped. No wonder Molly had laughed.

She glanced back to be sure Molly hadn't followed her to laugh some more. She hadn't, so Jinky separated the tree branches to get a closer look. Beside the stone girl was a small statue of a doe with its open mouth raised to the dipper the girl held.

Jinky stooped to read the words printed on the base of the statue. VIRGINIA DARE AND DOE. When Jinky straightened, her face was exactly level with the stone girl's, and she whispered, "To think I was scared half out of my wits by you, Pete's sake. I guess I was pretty dumb to think *you* could leave footprints!" Automatically Jinky looked down at the soft earth around the statue.

But there *were* footprints!—over there on the side where she had not stepped yet—and they were not Molly's either, because they had been made by sneakers, and Molly didn't even own a pair.

There, back behind Jinky's own, were Molly's prints. Molly's heel print was separated from the sole and went deeper, the way her saddle oxfords would.

Eagerly Jinky stepped across to the stranger's footprints. She pressed her own shoe into the sand beside them. She felt like a detective herself as she examined the two side by side.

The prints left by the intruder had a peanut-shaped mark in the middle of the sole that was probably from a worn place, otherwise they were exactly like Jinky's. They must have been made by a girl's shoes, Jinky decided. A boy's shoes would be wider.

The noise she had thought she heard as she stood here last night might have been made by someone hiding *behind* the statue. But who? And why?

Molly can keep her old ghost. I'm going to keep looking for clues, Jinky vowed, until I find the real live person who made these footprints. Maybe that person will even turn out to be friendly. Then I'll have someone to talk to who doesn't go around blabbing everything the way Molly does.

Jinky jumped as Duke and Baron bounded up without warning, scattering the footprints. She guessed it didn't matter that they were gone, since she wasn't going to tell Molly about them and wouldn't need them for proof. She *was* glad to see the dogs.

Baron sat down beside the statue. But Duke ran circles around Jinky, enticing her to play.

She didn't get a chance, though, because Mother called from the front door to come eat breakfast this minute.

Jinky hurried to mind her and was thankful when Mother didn't scold about last night's eavesdropping as she handed her her plate of kept-warm breakfast. But Jinky noticed that Mother's face had a faraway worried look. She knew it was because of Father. A dark cloud settled over the place where Jinky's appetite should have been.

It was even harder to eat as Jinky listened to Mother call a Dr. Forrest on the old-fashioned kitchen wall phone. It turned out that the doctor wanted to see Father that afternoon.

Mother had no more finished worrying aloud, "I hope the moving truck gets here with his crutches before the time for his appointment," than the wish seemed magically granted. The dogs began barking, and when they all looked out the window to see why, there was their moving van stopping in the drive.

Glad for an excuse to stop eating, Jinky ran to let the dogs know it was all right. The van seemed much smaller here where everything was so open. She bet those men watching her walk right up to the ferociously barking dogs were thinking she was as brave as a soldier.

Both dogs hushed the very second Jinky called, "Duke! Baron!" the way she'd heard Father do last night.

Jinky touched Baron's head gratefully. "Good boy!" She'd thought Duke would mind her, but she hadn't been so sure about Baron. Now they really were her dogs. She walked between them as she led the moving men up to the house for instructions from Mother.

"For the time being," Mother explained, "we'll store everything except the clothes and books out here." She led them to a long, empty glassed-in porch behind the kitchen which Jinky hadn't even known existed.

There were so many things about this house she didn't know. But she had no chance to explore, because Mother asked her and Molly to help hang clothes in closets, and stack books, and find a place to keep their bikes. Mother looked first of all for Father's crutches and took them up to him.

Then, by the time the truck was gone and they had a quick lunch, it was time to take Father, who had eaten in his room, to the doctor's office.

Jinky walked into the living room just as Father hobbled slowly down the stairs. His thin shoulders were hunched because of the crutches.

Jinky saw with a sinking heart that one of Father's trouser legs was empty. She knew this meant he couldn't even wear his artificial leg. The only time Father went without it was when the place just above where his knee should have been, caused him great pain. Jinky turned away quickly for fear he might think she was staring or something, Pete's sake.

She tried to shut out the shuffle-clomp sound of his foot and the crutches by humming noisily. She pretended to be very busy tilting the platform rocker as far forward as it would go, then letting it flop back on its creaky hinges.

All the time she creaked the rocker, Jinky was remembering way back when she'd been little and had longed to be like her father. She hadn't been able to make her voice sound deep like his, nor shave off whiskers every morning, but she *could* limp the way he did—and had, until Mother caught her.

Mother had not understood at all. She sat Jinky down in a straight-backed chair and talked to her a long time about how wrong it was to make fun of people who had a handicap.

Jinky had not understood Mother either, and wondered where Father kept his "handy cap," and why he never wore it.

Now that she was older she knew what Mother meant. Jinky often thought of trying to explain, especially to Father, that she had thought limping was a wonderful way to walk. That she had not been making fun of him, only trying to be like him. But she knew she'd never get up the courage to say it.

At last Jinky heard Mother say, "There. The steps down from the porch will be easier."

It was only a few minutes' drive to Nag's Head. On the way Molly pointed out things she'd seen that morning. The ocean was astonishingly big and had a tremendous roar, considering what gentle-looking waves of it lapped onto the endless beach.

Father seemed more like himself now that he was sitting in the car. He motioned toward a smooth stretch of sand and said, "Once, when I was young, my mother brought my brother Joe and me to this beach to play. We climbed sand dunes and pretended to be pirates digging for Blackbeard's treasure. This is actually where it is supposed to be buried. In those days you could still see the skeletons of old ships wrecked along the shore and half buried in the sand."

And in those days, Jinky thought with a little ache,

Father had two good legs, and his brother Joe was alive, and his mother, too. She wondered if when Father and Uncle Joe were boys they used to quarrel all the time the way she and Molly did. And if they did, she wondered if it made Father sad to think about it now.

"What did Uncle Joe look like?" Molly asked.

Father tapped his cold pipe against his palm. "Much more like me than you look like Jinky. We did everything together. Even went off to war at the same time. Only Joe went into the Air Corps and was a fighter pilot over Germany, where he was killed the same year you girls were born. I was sent to the Pacific with the Marines."

This was the most Jinky could remember Father talking about the war. She saw the clothesline look pass between Mother and him as he went on. "I think it's about time we tell the girls about Joe's marriage to—"

"Jim, we're almost there," Mother interrupted as if she wished he'd talk about something else. Jinky guessed this was because Mother thought the whole story was too sad to talk about with Father sick and all.

Soon they stopped in front of the doctor's office.

Jinky and Molly were to wait in the car. As soon as the folks had gone, Molly began pointing out things she'd seen earlier. "The main street is named Virginia Dare," she said, "so you can see they must still believe in her ghost."

Jinky couldn't see how that proved anything, but she didn't feel much like talking.

Jinky decided the little town looked friendly enough. She liked the way everything, even the buildings, seemed to be a part of the ocean and sand and openness. If only Father were well, she guessed it might be a pretty nice place to live.

The longer the folks were gone, the more worried Jinky felt. She only half listened to Molly, who was saying, "You know, Jinky, this town is our birthplace the same as Virginia Dare's. Mother told me this morning about how during the war she came here to be near Grandmother Smith because Father was gone and she had no one else—"

"Here they come now," Jinky interrupted as the door to the office opened.

A NEW WORRY

Anxiously Jinky watched Father balance himself with the crutches. She waited as he opened the car door, not daring to ask what the doctor had said.

Father slid into the front, propped the clumsy crutches against the back of the seat, and slammed his door.

Mother, who seemed to be having trouble finding the car keys in her purse, said, "The doctor says everything is going to be all right, but—"

But what? Jinky's heart did a flip which seemed to land it in her throat.

"What your mother means," Father said matter-of-factly, "is that I've injured my hip, but it's nothing serious."

Jinky watched Mother smooth and resmooth a pleat in her yellow skirt. "He has to go to a special clinic back across on the mainland right away, tomorrow morning. The doctor wants him to fly instead of riding so far in a car. There's a small plane which will take us from Nags Head."

Jinky swallowed hard. "Will we—Will all of us go?"

Mother looked at Jinky. "That's just it," she said. "You girls will have to stay here. It will only be for two days and one night if all goes well. The doctor said I could sleep on a cot in Father's room, but—" Then she looked at Molly. "You can see that you girls couldn't stay there, too."

"Sure." Molly was so cheerful that Jinky could have punched her in the nose.

"I explained to the doctor," Mother went on, "that I had no one to leave you with. He told us about a woman who—well her name is Miss Weatherspoon. The doctor has known her all his life. He says she often stays with Banker children."

"Banker children?" Molly asked. To Jinky she sounded as if finding out what Banker children were was more important than learning that Father had to go to that clinic. Molly isn't even worried, Jinky thought. Why can't *I* feel the way she does?

Father turned to answer Molly's question. So he wouldn't see her tears, Jinky ducked down, pretending her sneaker lace needed tying.

"They call everyone a Banker who was born on the Outer Banks—out here beyond the Sound," Father said. "They call everyone else comers 'n' goers."

So that's why the man who brought the telegram called himself a Banker, Jinky thought, untying and slowly retying the other lace. And he had said Mr. McLeod's widow wasn't exactly a Banker or a comer 'n' goer. But this woman, this Miss Weatherspoon, she would be a Banker. Would she believe that Virginia Dare's ghost roamed the sand dunes every night?

Jinky swiped at her eyes and straightened up—too soon, because Father was watching her thoughtfully. She was ashamed of the way her heart jumped as he turned to Mother and said, "Why don't I go alone and you stay with the girls?"

"Absolutely not," Mother said, and even though Jinky's hopes plunged again, she was glad Mother said it. "Before we'll let you go through this alone," Mother added, "we'll take the girls along and find someone on the mainland to leave them with."

That would be much better, Jinky thought, re- membering how Emmet Saunders had said Mr. Mc- Leod was murdered in that house. Jinky wondered if Molly, who had been half asleep when she told her, remembered *that*.

Jinky watched Father shake his head. "No, they'd be better off here at—home." The way he said home made Jinky ache for him. Was he sorry now they had moved clear out here? Was the secret reason important enough to be worth all this?

And she ached for herself too, but not for Molly. Pete's sake, it seemed like Molly was trying to make everyone notice that Jinky was miserable about the folks leaving, because she said, "You aren't supposed to bite your fingernails, Jinky." Then she added, "I think it will be lots of fun to stay here with Miss Weatherspoon."

Jinky saw Mother look at Molly gratefully. She tried to turn the corners of her own mouth up to make everyone think she agreed with Molly. But her lips felt like cardboard.

And her mouth went dry as cardboard, too, when Molly said, "I wonder if this Miss Weatherspoon has ever seen the ghostly bloodstain where—"

Jinky groaned. Pete's sake, Molly had thought of nothing but ghosts since they moved here.

"This is a *different* legend"—Molly gave Jinky a long look—"but from the same book. This one's the legend of an everlasting stain in the sand on a beach around here, from the blood of a woman slain by her husband who found her in the arms of another and didn't wait to hear that the stranger was her long-lost brother. I'm going to ask Miss Weatherspoon if she knows where that stain is!"

"Molly, I wish—" Jinky began.

"And there's another Nags Head legend, too," Molly went on, "about a headless horseman who gallops over the sand dunes—"

"Molly!" Mother's smile softened her scolding voice. "The doctor told us some good news, too. If you'll give me a chance, I'll tell you about it."

Even Mother doesn't want to hear all that stupid stuff about ghosts, Jinky thought. It was okay for Molly to act so brave about staying with this strange woman. Getting acquainted with grownups was practically her hobby—grownups *and* legends. Jinky wished she never had to hear the word legend again.

What she wanted to hear now was the good news Mother had.

"It seems," Mother explained, flipping the key to start the car, "there's been a big improvement in making artificial legs, and they fit them at this clinic. They use a stronger, lighter material, which means no shoulder straps—makes it easier to walk."

Mother suddenly slowed the car. "I think," she said, "we'd all feel more satisfied if we settled our plans as soon as possible. Why don't we go to Miss Weatherspoon's house now? The rest of you can wait in the car while I talk with her. If I see that she will do, we can make definite arrangements."

Father agreed, and Jinky crossed two fingers on each hand and hid them under her knees. She won't do! She won't do! she wished as hard as she could.

While Mother drove slowly down Virginia Dare Street, the road they had used to come into town, the folks discussed directions the doctor had given them to find Miss Weatherspoon's house.

Molly helped by reading off street signs and house numbers. But Jinky just stared miserably out her window at the dancing whitecaps that topped the ocean as far out as she could see and ended in scalloped sheets on the beach. I hope she can't speak English and that she's dirty as a pig and . . .

Jinky's shoulder pressed the side of the car as it turned away from the ocean onto a deserted narrow road. About three blocks up that road they stopped in front of a small weathered cottage.

The front window shades were pulled, giving the house a secretive look. A faded American flag drooped from a pole slanting out from the roof. Near the door a porch swing dangled by one chain. Except for two scraggy pine trees, there was only gray sand in the yard.

The place looked bleak and ugly. Jinky suspected gloomily that this Miss Weatherspoon would match the house she lived in.

Mother smoothed her dark hair in the rear-view mirror and gave them all a reassuring smile before she marched up to the front porch. She had no more knocked on the door than it opened a crack as if someone had been watching from behind it. Soon the door opened a bit wider and Mother disappeared.

Jinky huddled in her corner and tried not to be envious as Molly and Father got into one of their discussions. They talked about things that used to be around here years ago: land pirates, herds of wild Banker ponies, and something called the Great Dismal Swamp, which was still here.

When the folks get back from this trip, Jinky thought desperately, and things settle down, I'm going to find out where the library is. I'm going to start at one end of the top shelf and read every book in the place.

She felt like a selfish, miserable lump for hoping Miss Weatherspoon wouldn't "do," and she wished she could simply vanish!

To pass the time, Jinky stared at the shabby flag

and recited the Pledge of Allegiance over and over in her mind. She was on "republic for which it stands" when Mother came back out the door. Jinky watched Mother's face.

Before Mother was halfway across the yard, Jinky could tell. She'll *do,* she thought, slumping back on the car seat and letting her fingers uncross.

But then, just in case there was still a chance Miss Weatherspoon would not do, Jinky whisked her hands behind her back and triple-crossed three fingers.

Mother's first words dashed Jinky's last hopes.

GIRL SPY

"I like Miss Weatherspoon," Mother announced, "and I hope you'll all agree when I tell you about her. I would have asked her to come out to meet you, but she was wearing her hat when I went in, so I'm sure she was planning to go someplace."

"What's she like?" Molly asked eagerly.

"Peppy and nice." Mother started the car. "And, Jim, she knew your mother. She knows Mrs. McLeod, too, the lady who owns our house."

"Good recommendations," Father said.

Mother's answer made Jinky lean forward anxiously.

"She didn't exactly give Mrs. McLeod's name as a recommendation," Mother said thoughtfully. "In fact, something she said gave me the impression that Mrs. McLeod and Miss Weatherspoon had once been very close friends, but that something, some kind of trouble, maybe a tragedy, had come between them."

"A mystery!" Molly cried. "Maybe she'll tell us about that. Maybe it has something to do with Mr. McLeod's murd—" Molly clapped her hand over her mouth and rolled her eyes toward Jinky.

So Molly had not been too sleepy to remember. Now I'm going to get it! Jinky thought in the sudden silence.

But much to Jinky's surprise Mother glanced over her shoulder and said, "Now, Molly, don't try to make something out of nothing. Just because Miss Weatherspoon is the kind of person who says exactly what she thinks doesn't mean she is involved in a mystery. She was very fond of your grandmother. I have the feeling that when we get back you two will have made her your first friend in Nags Head."

Molly will, Jinky thought, making fists inside her jeans pockets, but I won't.

"I know I'll like her," Molly said, and Jinky could just *feel* her sister already thinking up ways to get in good with Miss Weatherspoon.

They turned back onto the main road, and Jinky saw that now a distant fog was beginning to blot out the whitecaps on the ocean. She wondered if the fog would keep rolling ghostlike toward the shore, then across the sand until it shrouded the Yaupon Moat house again tonight.

If it does, she thought, maybe the fog will make the others feel as lonely as I do. Then maybe the folks will change their minds and take Molly and me along, even if we have to sit all night in a waiting room.

Pete's sake, even that would be better than staying here with some strange old woman.

But Jinky's hopes dimmed as she caught the tail end of Mother's sentence: ". . . and Miss Weatherspoon said she could get Emmet Saunders to drive her to our house in the morning. It's all going to work out fine. He can drive us in to the landing strip on the other side of Nags Head and meet us there when we return."

Everyone is trying to make the best of Father's illness except me, Jinky thought guiltily. She skidded the sole of her sneaker back and forth across the gritty pages of a comic book she'd left on the floor of the car. She felt worse than if she'd struck out when her team was losing an important game.

A while later when they were all back inside the kitchen of the Yaupon Moat house, Mother telephoned Miss Weatherspoon to say they wanted her to come for *sure*.

"You know," Mother said as she hung the receiver back on the wall phone, "Miss Weatherspoon's voice sounded different. I even asked twice if it *was* Miss Weatherspoon."

Father said something about old cable lines changing the sound of a voice, but Jinky didn't really hear, because she had to get out of there before she started blubbering in front of everyone.

She let the kitchen door swing shut and stumbled through the house and out the front door. Nobody was going to see her bawl, Pete's sake!

Outside, the air was already damp with fog. It smelled like the salty sea and ancient fishbones. Duke ran up and licked Jinky's hand as if he wanted to offer sympathy. "Good boy," she whispered.

Jinky and Duke followed the steppingstones until they reached the tree where the Virginia Dare statue stood. Jinky led the way through the bushes to the stone maiden. She nudged her toe against a matchstick-thin leg of the white doe. "At least I'm not scared of this any more," she whispered. "Petes sake, I—"

Jinky stopped short. She stared in amazement at the ground. On the sandy earth around the base of the statue were more of those same footprints!

Whoever made those footprints must have come back while she and her family were in Nags Head.

Jinky dropped to her knees. Sure enough, there was that same peanut-shaped worn place. And she was positive now that these were the prints of a girl's shoe —a girl about her own age. Excited tingles pricked her shoulders. Jinky stood up and listened carefully. She could hear no sound except the faint far cry of a sea gull. Or was that a rustling?

She tipped her head back to search the twisty leaf-covered limbs above her. Nothing in sight. The rustling must have been made by a squirrel or a bird.

Jinky tore through the scrubby bushes and looked from one end of the yard to the other. The mystery person had disappeared.

With Duke bounding along beside her, she dashed to the back of the house. From here she could see all the way to a line of barrier dunes sprigged with spiky grass stalks. No one. But those bushes down by the moat would be a perfect place to hide and spy.

I'll bet that's just what she's doing, Jinky thought as she scrambled toward the moat—spying on us. Jinky rather liked the idea. Spying was sort of like eavesdropping. Even if neither one was considered very nice, both were a good way to learn things.

Jinky found herself admiring the mystery girl without ever having seen her. One thing sure, she was not afraid of dogs—coming around here when the place was deserted. And she wore sneakers instead of prissy saddle oxfords like Molly.

Jinky crossed the flat bridge and searched down the back side of one row of yaupon bushes, then the other. Nobody here. The girl must have run when she heard their car. But where does she live? Jinky wondered. Who is she? Why doesn't she want us to see her?

Suddenly Jinky felt as if she would burst if she didn't tell someone about the mysterious footprints. Should she share her secret with Molly?

There was no one else. Back home she had plenty of friends, most of them boys. Boys did not go around telling everything you told them. She pounded her fist into her palm. Still, if Molly had a real mystery like this one to help solve, she might forget about those silly ghosts of hers.

But Jinky had no chance to tell Molly about the footprints. When she started for the house, she saw Molly on the front porch beckoning her to hurry.

"It's important," Molly called, and Jinky forgot the mystery girl. Was Father worse? She sighed with relief when Molly said, "Mother wants to talk to us right now in the kitchen while she starts supper." Molly grabbed Jinky's hand and pulled her toward the door. "I think she's going to tell us the secret!"

It *was* about the secret that Mother wanted to talk. "I realize," she began as she floured a drumstick and dropped it into a pan of sizzling grease, "that you girls know your father and I had a special reason for moving to this town. Stay back. This might pop!"

Jinky backed off. "Where is he?"

"Your father? He's upstairs resting. I'm going to take supper up to him." Mother shook salt on the drumstick, then ground pepper from a little pepper box. "First of all, I want you to know that the only reason we kept this a secret was that, until the telegram came last night, we weren't sure about—Well even now I can't . . ."

Mother shook her head. "You girls are simply going to have to understand that we will have to wait until Father feels up to talking about this with us."

Jinky felt sorry for Mother. She had never seen her act so mixed up. "It's okay," Jinky said.

Mother took a deep breath and jabbed a piece of chicken with the long-handled fork. "When things are important—so important they may change quite a few people's lives—they have to be handled properly. Your father and I planned so carefully, but"—she eyed Jinky—"we didn't expect our plans to be overheard by certain people before we were ready to tell them.

Nor could we have known that we'd have to be gone
from here for two days. Do you understand?"

"I understand," Molly said quickly. "Just tell us if
it has anything to do with a ghost or not."

"Ghost?" A brief smile crossed Mother's lips.
"Well, since you are so fond of ghost stories, honey, I
guess you could say it does, in a way."

Jinky chewed her thumbnail. Why hadn't Mother
laughed right out loud and told Molly there was no
such thing as a ghost? "What—? kind of a ghost?"
she demanded anxiously.

Mother put her hand on Jinky's shoulder. "I can
never please both of you. I guess I didn't mean a *solid*
ghost, Jinky. I meant like a ghost out of the past. Now
no more questions."

"You mean like—" Jinky began.

"Jinky!" Mother interrupted, "Don't try to guess,
as if it were some kind of a riddle. You know if *you*
hadn't eavesdropped—"

Jinky could tell that Mother's patience was nearly
gone. But she could not leave things the way they
were. "Pete's sake, I didn't mean to eavesdrop. Can't
you go ahead and—"

"Jinky!"

"Sorry." Jinky looked sideways at Molly. She could
tell from her smug look that Molly thought she had
this all figured out. Molly thought she was right in the
first place—that the secret *did* have something to do
with Virginia Dare's ghost wandering over the dunes
every night.

I wish, Jinky thought desperately, I'd never eavesdropped and heard about this dumb old secret. She turned away, feeling suddenly cross at the whole world. With both hands flat she hit the swinging door hard and stomped through it.

She dropped down onto the bottom step and sat, chin in hand, listening to Mother and Molly chattering in the kitchen. In a little bit Molly came in and said importantly, "Let me past so I can carry Father's supper up."

After supper, when Mother, Molly, and Jinky had finished the dishes, Mother said, "I want everyone to get right to bed. It's been a hard day and we have to get up early."

Jinky and Molly climbed the stairway side by side. Jinky looked across Molly's shoulder to where their shadows blended together, stalking them like a wide crooked ghost, and she shuddered. If the house seemed this scary tonight with Mother and Father still here, how would it seem tomorrow night, with only that Banker woman?

Still, even with the sinister fog hovering near the long low window, their bedroom seemed cozier than it had last night. The canopy-covered poster beds looked snug and safe in the soft light from the petticoat lamp.

Jinky stretched under the quilts and thought about the footprints. Now would be a good time to tell Molly about them.

She watched Molly putting her dress neatly on a hanger. She thought about the way Molly had acted last night when she told her about the girl—or rather, about the statue, as it turned out. Jinky sure didn't want to hear another ghost story. But then, not even Molly could twist ordinary footprints around to make them sound as if they were made by a ghost.

Molly turned her own bedding down and scooted underneath. Jinky had almost made up her mind to tell Molly, when Molly surprised her by saying, "I'll stay awake tonight until you go to sleep—for nothing."

"Pete's sake!" Jinky cried thankfully. "I'll hurry." The story of the mystery girl could wait until morning. She let her eyelids close. At least when the folks were gone she'd have Molly. And she'd have the dogs. It might not be so bad after all. And Father would be well again soon, even better than ever with that new kind of leg.

Jinky snuggled deeper into the covers. First thing tomorrow she would tell Molly about the mystery girl's footprints.

MISS WEATHERSPOOK

Before she opened her eyes the next morning, Jinky thought about the folks leaving. She rolled over to see if Molly was awake yet. The same as yesterday morning, her sister's bed was empty.

All sorts of worries began tumbling into Jinky's head as she got up and started pulling on the clothes she had dropped in a heap on the rocker last night.

The minute the folks leave, she decided, I'll tell Molly about the footprints. That will take her mind off asking Miss Weatherspoon about those Nags Head ghosts.

For all I know, Jinky thought, the girl who left those tracks by the statue might be hiding out there right now. I wonder where Molly is. Suddenly Jinky realized she hadn't heard a sound throughout the house since she woke up. Taking a chance on Mother being too busy with the trip to notice, she smoothed her hair with her hands and hurried out of her room.

Her rubber soles squeaked on the hall floor as she

ran toward the steps. Even in broad daylight Jinky
hated being the only one in the upstairs part of this
house.

She felt better when she found Molly and Mother
in the kitchen. Molly was setting the table. Jinky saw
that her sister had fixed her hair a special way. Instead
of her usual ponytail she had brushed it smooth and
left it down long with a little bow behind one ear.

Molly had on a fresh white blouse buttoned up
high at the neck and her blue plaid gathered skirt.
Jinky looked down at her own rumpled jeans and
baggy sweatshirt. Molly wants to impress that old
Banker woman, she thought darkly.

Mother had a tea towel tied over the skirt of her
good black suit. She was arranging dishes on a yellow
tray. "Morning, Jinky," she said as she spooned hot
grits onto one of the plates. "Soon as I take this upstairs, I'll—"

"Is Father worse?"

"No, I just want to save him those steps."

So she hadn't been alone up there after all. Jinky
was glad nobody knew how she'd hurried. "I'll carry
it to him," she offered.

"No," Mother answered so quick and sharp that
Jinky, who had already reached for the tray, almost
tripped over her own feet.

"Sorry, honey," Mother apologized, "I guess I'm
all nerves this morning. It's just that I want you to
eat now, so we can get the dishes finished before I
leave."

Jinky couldn't help wondering if Mother would

have said yes if Molly had asked to carry Father's breakfast to him. Everybody treated Molly as if she were practically grown up.

Jinky looked at the two plates of breakfast Molly was carrying over to the table. The plate with one piece of toast cut into ladylike wedges was Molly's, of course. The one heaped with grits and eggs and crispy bacon would be Jinky's. Molly had a cup of tea, too. Molly pretended to hate milk, but Jinky knew Molly really thought that drinking tea was more grown up.

Jinky sat down in front of the full plate. She had to admit she was hungry—even if this was probably going to be the worst day in her life.

A while later, when they were doing dishes, Mother gave last-minute instructions. Mostly they were don't's, but finally she said, "If you will be very careful, and if it's all right with Miss Weatherspoon, you may ride your bikes into town. That should be fun."

Jinky's spirits lifted. That *would* be fun. And maybe along the way they would see the spying mystery girl.

"And Molly," Mother went on, "you helped put the groceries away yesterday, so you show Miss Weatherspoon where things are—" Mother stopped suddenly as the sound of a car's motor came through the open kitchen window. "That must be Emmet Saunders now." Mother tossed her tea-towel apron on a chair and hurried through the door with Molly behind her.

The door no more swung shut than it opened again and Father, hunched on his crutches, stuck his head in.

"Jinky," he said, "run up and get those two over-night bags by our bed."

"Sure!" Jinky was pleased to get a chance to do something for Father before he left.

When she was halfway up the steps, Father called, "And bring my billfold and change from the dresser. I forgot them."

Jinky ran to the folks' bedroom. She scooped up the change. But as she reached for Father's billfold she saw beside it another small white card like the one still in her shoe.

She glanced over her shoulder to make sure she was alone, then picked up the second card and read:

MRS. AGNES MOONEY, DIRECTOR

SUNSHINE HOME

Nothing important, Jinky decided, sliding the card on top of the billfold. She grabbed up the light bags and hurried downstairs.

Mother, Father, and Molly were already starting toward the front hall. "I'll carry the bags out to the car," Jinky said as she caught up with Father to give him his billfold and change.

As Jinky dropped the card into Father's hand, she saw him look quickly at Mother.

Mother stopped in the middle of pulling on her glove. "She's done it again," the clothesline look said. This time there wasn't a thing about the look that seemed cozy.

Jinky felt her cheeks burn. Father must have thought the card was inside his billfold. Did they think she had taken it out? And it must be important after all. It must be part of the secret.

She wished she had paid more attention to the woman's name. Mrs. Somebody at a Sunshine Home. But Jinky had no time to think any more about that, because Mother said, "Come on girls," and herded Jinky and Molly ahead of her. "I'll introduce you to Miss Weatherspoon."

Emmet Saunders' car was so faded you couldn't tell what color it had been. "Mornin', folks," he called out the window. "Nice weather for flyin' over to the mainland."

By the time they reached the car, a little old woman grasping a worn brown bag had climbed from the high back seat. She was wearing a wide-brimmed hat with cloth roses on it, and she was hardly any taller than Jinky herself.

"Miss Weatherspoon, this is Jinky," Mother said, putting her arm around Jinky's shoulder, "and this is Molly. Girls, this is Miss Weatherspoon."

Jinky stared into the sharpest pair of blue eyes she had ever seen. As the woman looked at Jinky, a flicker of surprise shot through those eyes. Her jaw dropped and Jinky thought she was going to say something, but she only nodded.

"The girls will tell you where things are," Mother said, "and they're to help when you need them."

Father shook hands with Miss Weatherspoon and then said they must get started. Mother told them to be good. "And, oh, yes," she added, "if you should need to call us, the number is on the ledge under the telephone."

Both girls kissed Mother and Father goodbye and everyone pretended everything was just fine, but Jinky was sure that it wasn't at all. She fought back tears as she watched the car bump across the bridge.

When there was nothing left to wave at but a cloud of dust, Jinky turned slowly around. To her surprise, the old lady was staring at her in a most peculiar way. Jinky quickly reminded herself that Mother had said they would like Miss Weatherspoon—even though that seemed impossible at this minute.

Jinky's elbows prickled as the little woman sailed right past Molly, set her squashy bag down, and put her bony hand on Jinky's shoulder.

Jinky forced herself to stand still while Miss Weatherspoon studied her from head to feet with those flinty eyes.

"She's Jinky, I'm Molly," Molly said at last from behind Miss Weatherspoon's shoulder. For once in her life Jinky was thankful to her sister for trying to get a grownup's attention.

But Miss Weatherspoon didn't even seem to hear Molly. Instead of answering she spun Jinky around and looked at her from all sides.

"We're twins," Molly tried again. This time her voice sounded desperate. "Fraternal twins—not identical. We just moved here yesterday, I guess Mother told you . . ." Molly's voice trailed away. She might as well have been talking to one of the yaupon bushes!

There was an awful silence while the old woman shook her head so hard her hat brim flapped. At last she opened her mouth to speak. With her first word, Jinky realized that up to now Miss Weatherspoon had not spoken once.

"I declare"—Miss Weatherspoon's voice was unusually loud with hardly any expression in it—"I've never seen the likes!"

Miss Weatherspoon moved her hand from Jinky's arm, and Jinky quickly backed off a step. What was wrong with this spooky old lady? With her eyes Jinky signalled Molly over Miss Weatherspoon's shoulder, "*Do* something!"

But Molly just rolled her own eyes and shrugged, palms up.

Jinky's skin still tingled under her sweatshirt sleeve from Miss Weatherspoon's touch. Somebody *had* to say something. Just as Jinky decided she could stand it no longer, a word came into her mind. It was her old baseball team's secret word. Would it give her courage now, the way it had back home? She decided to try it. "Poohw raw," she whispered.

It worked. Jinky suddenly felt almost as brave as a real Indian. She looked straight at Miss Weatherspoon and asked, "P-pardon me, but what haven't you seen the likes of?"

Jinky thought she saw the flicker of a smile in those steely eyes, but decided she was wrong when Miss Weatherspoon said, "I have a sort of a hospital in my house for—but never mind—you'll find out soon enough in a town this size." She flapped her hat brim once more. "Ask me no questions," she added, "and I'll tell you no lies." Then she picked up her wheezy bag and started off toward the house.

Jinky felt as if she were having a bad dream. She moved close to Molly, but kept watch on Miss Weatherspoon's retreating back. "Pete's sake, Molly," she whispered, "I don't—"

"If you ask me," Molly interrupted, "her name ought to be Weatherspook instead of spoon." Molly narrowed her eyes. "And I wish she was a spook, too, so she'd vanish!"

Jinky looked at her sister. Was Molly really mad, or was she scared and trying to hide it. Either way, Miss Weatherspoon was one grownup Molly was *not* going to be able to impress. Jinky had not realized until now how much she had counted on Molly to get acquainted for both of them.

Because there didn't seem to be anything else to do, they followed slowly behind Miss Weatherspoon.

Jinky noticed that Miss Weatherspoon limped a little and that one of her heavy black oxfords had an extra-thick sole. Her flowered silk dress reached almost to her shoe tops, and she was wearing a man's gray sweater which hiked up in the middle of the back.

The woman hobbled up the steps, crossed the porch, and disappeared through the front door. By the time Jinky and Molly had tiptoed into the house behind Miss Weatherspoon, she was heading straight up the stairs, still clutching her bag.

Clomp-step, clomp-step. Neither Jinky nor Molly

moved until Miss Weatherspoon was around the turn and out of sight. Then Jinky pulled Molly toward the kitchen so they could talk without being overheard.

"I don't like her," Molly said almost before the door stopped swinging.

"Remember," Jinky said, trying to sound hopeful, "Mother said we *would* when we got to know her. Why don't you—you know—*talk* to her when she comes down?"

"Ha!" Molly cried. "You heard me trying to." Jinky walked her fingers along the edge of the table. She tried hard not to look as miserable as she felt. "What do you think she meant when she said she had never seen the likes of me?"

"I don't know and I don't care." Molly flipped her skirt angrily and marched toward the back-porch door.

"Hey, wait!" Jinky didn't want to be trapped here alone with that woman. "What're you going to do?"

"Find my diary in one of the boxes," Molly said airily.

But her voice didn't fool Jinky. Molly never put anything down in her diary unless she was trying to figure it out. And it was always something important, too.

Molly stopped short with her hand on the porch doorknob, and both girls looked up as they heard clomp-step, clomp-step on the floor above.

"She sure knows her way around this house," Molly muttered.

"Probably"—Jinky tried to sound matter-of-fact— "probably Mother told her which room to use." But even as she said it, Jinky was thinking about Mother telling them that Miss Weatherspoon and Mrs. Mc-Leod *used* to be friends. But that some kind of trouble —"Molly!" Jinky gasped as she suddenly remembered something else Mrs. Weatherspoon had said. "What *kind* of a hospital do you suppose Miss Weatherspook—I mean spoon—has in her house?"

Molly's eyes widened and she shook her head slowly. Seeing Molly so upset made Jinky wish she had kept still about that hospital business.

"I know what we could do," Jinky said. "When Miss Weatherspoon comes back down, we'll ask her if we can ride our bikes to town. Then we'll go to her house and sort of spy. You know—sort of snoop around."

Talking about spying made Jinky remember the footprints and the mystery girl. But maybe now was the wrong time to tell Molly about that. Still, Jinky wished they knew the mystery girl. Maybe she would even turn out to be their friend. They could sure use a friend around here. "Molly," she began.

"Shhh," Molly warned, "here she comes. *You* ask her if we can go."

Jinky could hardly believe her ears. It was not like Molly to let anyone else do the talking. But, she reminded herself, the idea of going to spy on Miss Weatherspoon's house *had* been her own. And Molly must think it was a good plan. That made Jinky feel proud. Anyway there wasn't time to argue about who would ask, because the heavy footsteps were heading this way.

Jinky edged toward her sister as the door swung

open and Miss Weatherspoon came into the kitchen. "I hope you-all feel hungry," she announced loudly, "because I feel like cooking up a storm."

Why does she still have her hat on? Jinky wondered as she watched the woman's bony finger poke at a wisp of white hair that stuck out from under her wide-brimmed hat.

"Where," Miss Weatherspoon asked in her flat voice, "does your mama keep the yams?" Her bright eyes darted from Molly's face to Jinky's as if she intended to devour their words—if either dared speak up.

"Yams?" Jinky looked at her sister.

"Yams are sweet potatoes," Molly whispered, and for once she didn't act as if Jinky were dumb because she didn't know. "We bought some yesterday. They're in that bin over by the stove."

Jinky thought surely Miss Weatherspoon had heard Molly's stage whisper, but the old lady didn't move. What *was* the matter with her?

It was scary. But, Jinky decided, what worked once will work again. Poohw raw, she thought as hard as she could. Then she looked straight into Miss Weatherspoon's face.

Looking close this way, Jinky saw that the expression in those sharp eyes was definitely a lot more like worry than meanness. Miss Weatherspoon's eyes had a kind of a listening look, as if she expected—

All at once something clicked in Jinky's mind. She was almost sure she knew the reason this little old lady was acting so strangely. And if it turns out I'm wrong, Jinky thought, things can't be much worse. She faced Miss Weatherspoon and as clearly as she could said, "The-yams-are-in-that-bin-by-the-stove."

"I'm obliged," Miss Weatherspoon replied. Though her voice was flat as ever, her eyes said plenty. There was thankfulness in them, and a glimmer of something else, too. Like she and I have a secret, Jinky thought, feeling almost pleased.

Miss Weatherspoon went clomping over to the bin, and Jinky turned to her sister. "She's stone deaf!" Jinky said softly. "But she can read lips so well that I'll bet Mother didn't even know she can't hear."

Molly looked at Jinky with admiration. "That's why she didn't answer me out in the drive." She looked toward Miss Weatherspoon then back to Jinky. "But I still think she's peculiar. You ask her if we can ride into town."

Jinky hesitated. "It seems rude to leave so soon. Maybe I should talk to her about something else before I ask."

"Good idea," Molly agreed, giving Jinky a little shove.

Jinky walked slowly across the room and faced Miss Weatherspoon. She knew exactly what Molly would have said if she had been the one to do the talking, so she started off the same way. "Nags Head is certainly a nice town."

Miss Weatherspoon nodded agreeably, which encouraged Jinky. She watched Miss Weatherspoon dump a handful of the yams into the sink, then open a drawer and take out a paring knife. Miss Weatherspoon seemed to know exactly where the knives were kept. This gave Jinky an idea of what to say next.

"Mr. Emmet Saunders said not many people have seen the inside of this house. But I suppose Mrs. McLeod invited her friends—like you."

Miss Weatherspoon's heavy eyebrows shot up and she shook a few drops of water from her fingers. "I helped her move into this house," she said flatly.

Jinky began to worry for fear she had said the wrong thing. After all, there was that trouble Mother had mentioned. Jinky glanced across the room to Molly for help. Molly only nodded encouragingly.

"I guess"—Jinky plunged in again—"that Mr. McLeod was sure rich—to build a house like this. It's too bad he didn't get to live here before he was—" Jinky tried to think of a softer word, but "murdered" popped out.

The second she said it Jinky could see it was a bad mistake. Miss Weatherspoon's face began to turn bright red. That terrible word seemed to dangle in the air between them. Miss Weatherspoon clenched the knife tighter in her blue-veined hand. Sparks of anger lit her eyes as she cried at last, "Wicked. Wicked, you hear?"

For a minute the old woman rocked herself from side to side as if she were suffering a pain. Jinky would have run right out of this house, but where could she run to? And anyway her dumb feet seemed stuck to

the floor the same way they had seemed to be stuck to the dark path that first night. She was trapped.

A little sob started way down in Jinky's throat. She swallowed it back and thought, Poohw raw, harder than ever before.

Just when it seemed they were all going to stand frozen in these spots forever, Miss Weatherspoon's face began to change. It settled slowly back into that sort of gloomy-cheerful look it had before. "What's done is done," she said loudly. Then she pulled her mouth into a straight line as if she didn't intend to say one more word. With a little snort she picked up one of the yams and began to slash away the thick brownish-orange skin.

BEACONS AND LANTERNS

Jinky looked to make sure Molly was still there. She saw that Molly was signaling frantically for her to ask about the bike ride.

Shaking inside, Jinky leaned toward the sink so Miss Weatherspoon would see she had something more to say and blurted, "Mother said we could ride our bikes to town, can—may we?"

For a dreadful moment Miss Weatherspoon's sharp eyes seemed to be seeing straight into Jinky's mind, seemed to be seeing that Jinky was planning to go to Miss Weatherspoon's own house and snoop around.

Jinky was relieved when the old woman nodded and said, "I reckon, if your mama really said so. Mind you're careful. Don't stay too late, because the wind's making up in the northeast." Then Miss Weatherspoon laid down the yam and the knife. She shook her finger at Jinky. "You'd better stop mistaking lanterns for beacons, child," she said, "or you're going to get into a peck of trouble!"

Lanterns? Beacons? Jinky backed away. The words made no sense to her.

They must not have made sense to Molly either, because as soon as the twins had escaped and closed the heavy front door behind them, Molly asked, "What kind of trouble did she mean?"

Jinky almost giggled in spite of everything. *Molly* asking *her* what something meant! She put her arm across Molly's shoulder. With lots more confidence than she felt, Jinky said, "We'll feel better after we find out about that hospital business."

"Maybe we'll feel *worse!*" Molly cried, rolling her eyes.

"That doctor who told Mother about Mrs. Weatherspoon must know about her hospital," Jinky reminded Molly, "so it can't be too scary."

"I'm not so sure." Molly looked thoughtfully back at the big house. She hugged the tops of her arms and shivered. "Now I know how Alice felt when she finally got out of Wonderland! Maybe Miss Weatherspoon is a witch in disguise."

"Let's go," Jinky urged. She was afraid Molly would start telling about some book she'd read that said there really were such things as witches.

Their bikes were parked at the back of the house under two myrtle bushes which were almost as big as trees. Jinky glanced up at the kitchen window, a few inches too high to see into, and wondered if Miss Weatherspoon was watching them.

The dogs waited impatiently for the girls to get

started so they could escort them down the drive. As Jinky and Molly rode their bikes onto the moat bridge, a sudden strong wind smelling of the ocean tossed their hair and ballooned Molly's full skirt.

"Come on, boy," Jinky called to Duke and sped off the bridge ahead of her sister. All at once she had an idea. "Maybe Miss Weatherspoon's hospital is a rest home," she called back over her shoulder. "Maybe Mr. McLeod died there, and Mrs. McLeod blames Miss Weatherspoon. That could be the reason she got mad when I said he was murdered."

"Maybe," Molly called out above the wind, but she sounded doubtful.

Duke and Baron stopped at the hedgerow. The girls turned onto the smooth highway. The wind was at their backs for a while and their bikes whizzed along.

But further on, past a bend in the road, the wind whipped Jinky's hair back from her face and in the distance she saw that it was slashing like an invisible knife at the sea oat on the dunes.

Their bike tires made a singing sound on the pavement. All kinds of thoughts went around in Jinky's head as they passed the salt marsh. The swamp marsh hadn't seemed so spooky from the car window. It was edged with dark gray rushes, and deeper back all the taller growing things were hung with strands of witch's moss.

Jinky thought the marsh looked like the kind of place the ghost of Virginia Dare might use to wait for the stroke of midnight so it could become visible. She shivered and began to pedal harder.

Now the ocean came in sight. Jinky was startled again at how big it was—how much tumbling, turning water. What keeps it, she wondered, from simply rolling over the whole world? Sand blew into her eyes and mouth and she could taste salt. "How much farther?" she hollered back at Molly.

"We're about halfway," Molly answered. "There aren't any cars coming. Let's ride on that side now."

Before long Molly pointed ahead to where the lane-like road met the highway. On a bicycle the sandy road seemed more uphill than it had when they were in the car. Pumping hard, they topped a little rise, and there was Miss Weatherspoon's deserted-looking house.

Jinky and Molly stopped and stood astraddle their bikes to catch their breath. Jinky thought the house looked even more lonely than it had the first time. And it *did* match its owner. The wind whipped the faded flag and made the sagging porch swing creak as if it were being tortured by an invisible hand.

"Hey! Look!" Molly cried out so suddenly that Jinky almost dropped her bike.

Jinky's mouth went dry. She gripped her handle-bars. "What? Where?"

Molly pointed. "Over there."

"Pete's sake," Jinky sighed. It was nothing but a scrawny black and white kitten.

The half-starved kitten scampered up close to the

front of the house. But even with that much protec-
tion, the wind ruffled its fur. The kitten hunched its
rear legs until it was almost in a sitting position.

"Poor thing," Molly cried. "I'm going to rescue it."
Before she finished saying this, Molly was off her bike
and three-fourths of the way across the bare yard.

Jinky dropped her own bike and ran after Molly.
"He probably belongs to somebody," she called,
"maybe even to Miss Weatherspoon. Say! That's it!"
Jinky stopped short. "I'll bet she has a hospital for
animals!"

Molly was too busy trying to catch the cat to answer. The minute the kitten saw her swooping down
on him, he made a wild dash for the corner of the
house.

Each time Molly got a few feet from the kitten, he
gathered his tiny strength and ran again. Jinky began
to get the creepy feeling someone was watching all
this. From somewhere out of sight a hound dog
mourned louder than the wailing wind. Jinky ran to
catch up with Molly.

The kitten, which had led Molly all the way to the
back door, wavered now and almost toppled over. Just
as Molly reached for him, the cat scrambled along a
plank, up some sagging steps, and onto a small porch.

The porch was closed in with lattice boards and
was like a part of the house. Jinky thought surely
Molly would give up now. But Molly ran straight up
the steps, too, and disappeared behind the half-open
slatted door.

Jinky had no sooner put one foot onto the plank that led to the steps than she heard her sister gasp.

"What happened?" Jinky cried, her knees going weak.

"Quick! Come here!" Molly's voice was a mere squeak.

Jinky cleared the steps in two leaps. She found her sister pointing with a shaking finger at two wooden crates that took up almost half of the small stoop.

At first Jinky thought Molly was pointing at the cat, who was huddled pitifully between the boxes. The kitten's back was arched and he was spitting at them in fright.

But then Jinky's gaze moved from the rough floor, which looked as if it had never been swept by anything but the wind, to the lids of the boxes.

On one box, printed in large letters with heavy black crayon, was the word H E A D S. On the other was B O D I E S!

For one terrible second Jinky thought her wobbly knees were going to give way and let her fall right on top of those boxes. "M-Molly!" she heard her own voice croak.

Then even the wind seemed to catch its breath, and into the sudden silence came a new sound.

Jinky clutched at her sister in fresh terror as from behind them came the unmistakable creaking of a door being opened—slowly, slowly.

GHOST IN THE HOUSE

Whoever—or *whatever*—was opening that door was right behind them. Jinky stiffened. Any second now she expected something to reach out and grab her shoulders. Some dead leaves rustled against the lattice, and the sound beat like blackbird wings in her ears.

And then a quavery voice demanded, "What are you doing on my back porch?"

At least it was human. "Whew!" Jinky grabbed Molly's hand and without a backward look dragged her toward the rickety steps. But Molly's shoe caught on the last step and she fell sprawling across the plank.

Jinky stopped to pull Molly to her feet, and as she did she looked fearfully up at the porch.

The figure of an old woman filled the width of the doorway. Though she was fat, she was no taller than Miss Weatherspoon. The white apron pinned high on her dress hung clear to the floor. She wore rimless glasses so thick her eyes seemed to be a pale magnified blur. Why, she's nearly blind, Jinky thought. We must have scared her as much as she scared us.

The woman squinted down at Jinky, and her eyes almost disappeared into the deep wrinkles.

"Oh, it's you!" she said, much to Jinky's surprise. Then the woman put her hands on her wide hips. "Now why'd you come here today? Sister told you right out not to come again till she got back from keeping those Smith young'uns. Who's that girl with you? Why didn't you use the front door like you always do? Answer me, you hear?"

Jinky swallowed past the lump of fear that stuck in her throat. Had they discovered some horrible secret on that porch? And this woman claimed to be Miss Weatherspoon's sister, though Mother hadn't . . . And the woman thought she knew who Jinky was, but she didn't, because she'd said that about the Smith young'uns, and . . .

"I'm not—" Jinky began.

Molly nudged her. "Tell her we were just trying to catch that stray kitten."

"Kitten!" The old woman's voice snatched Molly's whispered word, and Jinky thought, She sure can *hear* better than our Miss Weatherspoon!

This new Miss Weatherspoon began searching the floor of the porch like an anxious mole. "Kitten? Kitten?" she repeated.

Apparently she did not see the kitten huddled between those awful boxes, because she shook her finger at Molly and said, "There's no cat around here. Whoever you are, child, you're mighty impertinent, trying to get Lily Joe to lie about what you were doing on my porch!"

Lily Joe? Jinky glanced at Molly to see what she made of *that*. But she could tell Molly was concentrating so hard on how to get hold of that cat that she hadn't even noticed.

Molly looked up at the woman. She squared her shoulders and put on a forced-looking smile. "Maybe we should introduce ourselves," she began in a trembly but polite voice. Just at that moment the kitten meowed.

The old woman cocked her head. "My land, there *is* a cat on this porch! Lily Joe, you march right back up here and carry it away. Brother is coming home any day now, and animals give him sneezing spells. He *is* coming home, you hear?" She sounded as if someone had said Brother was not coming home.

Molly nudged Jinky. "Go get him."

There didn't seem to be any way out of going back on that porch. On quicksand legs, Jinky started slowly up the steps. She kept a wary watch on the second Miss Weatherspoon as she edged herself down between the boxes. Somehow Jinky managed not to touch either box as she scooped up the cornered kitten.

She could feel its bones right through its thin fur. The kitten pinned its tiny claws into Jinky's sweatshirt as she hurried to get back to where Molly was.

The woman scolded her all the way down the steps. "You-all carry that cat down the road a piece and turn him loose. You know they won't let you keep an animal at the Home."

The Home? Something echoed in Jinky's mind. Sunshine Home! The name on Father's card! Was there some kind of a— Then suddenly another thought popped into her mind. Emmet Saunders had said that Mrs. McLeod gave all the money to build the new orphanage. So there *was* an orphanage here in Nags Head. Sometimes orphanages were called homes.

Could this Miss Weatherspoon, since she was practically blind, have mistaken Jinky for somebody named Lily Joe who lived in the orphanage. The real Lily Joe must come here often—only *she* used the *front* door!

Jinky unfastened the struggling kitten. She passed him into Molly's outstretched hands while the old woman warned, "Don't ever use this back door again, Lily Joe. You lettin' all that wind in just when I had things spread out for Sister to cut."

Cut! A picture of their Miss Weatherspoon's bony hand clutching the paring knife flashed through Jinky's mind. "Let's get out of here, Molly," she urged.

The kitten was quieter now that Molly held him. And Molly seemed a little more like her old self, too, as she managed to say goodbye almost as nicely as if they had been invited. But the second Miss Weatherspoon only scowled as they turned and ran.

Jinky's hands were so shaky she could barely lift up

her bike. We're in a worse mess than when we came here, she thought. We still don't know about the hospital in that house. And those boxes! Why did they have "heads" and "bodies" written on them?

She hopped onto her bike and hurried after Molly, who was riding away clutching the kitten with one hand and steering with the other.

As Jinky glanced back over her shoulder, she thought she saw the window shade behind the flag being raised a few inches. She shivered. Would that Miss Weatherspoon telephone her sister and tell her what she and Molly were up to? No, Jinky guessed, she won't do that, because she doesn't know who we really are. She kept calling me Lily Joe, whoever that is.

Halfway down the hill they raced past a man sweeping his sand yard with a broom. He waved. Jinky wondered if he, too, thought she was the girl called Lily Joe. "Are you okay?" she called to her sister.

"Yes," Molly shouted back, "but we'd better stop at the bottom of this hill so I can fix my cat to carry it more comfortably."

At the place where they would have turned back onto the highway toward home the girls braked their bikes to a halt and hopped off.

"Let's go over there," Molly said, pointing to the right a few yards. Leaning out of a sandy spot, almost hidden by a semicircle of wind-worried shrubs, was a sign that read, NAGS HEAD CITY LIMITS.

Molly held the struggling kitten with one hand while she and Jinky pushed their bicycles to this shelter at the edge of the highway. They dropped their bikes to the ground and flopped down after them.

"That awful woman!" Molly breathed. "Those awful boxes!"

"And she kept calling me Lily Joe!"

"That's because she couldn't see. She thought you were somebody else. But did you hear her say I was trying to make you lie about what we were doing on her porch!"

"Who do you suppose Lily Joe is?"

"Who cares as long as we got away and brought the kitten."

"What do you suppose she had spread out ready for her sister to cut?"

Molly took a deep breath. "Jinky, I've decided something. We are going to telephone the folks."

"We can't! Think how they'd worry." Jinky could see that her brave-sounding answer surprised Molly. The truth was it surprised her, too, since she'd been thinking about suggesting the same thing.

Molly hugged the kitten so hard he meowed in surprise. "Then what will we do?" she asked Jinky.

Once again Jinky thought how strange it seemed for Molly to be depending on her for answers. She felt almost dizzy with all that had happened since they moved here. Most of it was bad, of course, but still somehow she felt *older*. She even felt more like Molly herself, yet she hadn't *started* doing the things on her list! But right now she had to think of somebody who could help them.

"We could go to the police," she said. Then realizing that sounded too drastic, she added, "Or to Mrs. McLeod. She knows Miss Weatherspoon."

"Jinky," Molly said, petting the kitten with short rapid strokes, "I don't think you realize how serious this whole thing is. I read a story once . . ."

How can she think of stories at a time like this? Jinky wondered.

"This story," Molly continued in a low voice, "was called *Arsenic and Old Lace*. It was about two nice old ladies just like the Weatherspoon sisters—at least everyone *thought* they were nice. But they had a bad habit of killing people and hiding their bodies all around their house!"

"B-but Molly," Jinky stammered, suddenly feeling like her old worry-wart self again, "that was just a story."

"Father told me once that anything you wrote in a story had to be something that *could* happen in real life," Molly insisted. "The trouble with you, Jinky, is you don't realize that."

"Even if I did realize it, I still wouldn't like it." Jinky wished she and her family were back in their own little house in Centerville, where the worst thing that ever seemed to happen was that her team, the Indians, got beat now and then.

Molly pushed back her long hair and dabbed at her eye with a corner of her skirt. Molly hardly ever cried. Jinky knew this meant her sister was past being mad-scared and was getting just plain scared. And if they were this frightened now, in broad daylight, how would it seem when it got dark and they were shut up in that big house with one of the Weatherspoon sisters?

Molly sniffed, then held up her kitten with both hands. "Do you think the dogs will hurt my cat?" she asked in a small voice.

"The dogs! Why didn't I think of that before?" Jinky grabbed Molly's arm. "We can bring Duke and Baron inside to sleep in our bedroom. We'll be perfectly safe. Okay?"

"What if Miss Weatherspoon says we can't bring them in?"

Jinky could see that Molly thought her idea was a pretty good one. "I'll tell her that Mother said we could."

"That will be a lie."

"No it won't. You heard Mother tell us to take care of ourselves. That's what we'll be doing when we bring the dogs in."

"But those dogs probably know Miss Weatherspoon better than they do me." In spite of what she said, Molly didn't sound nearly as worried as she had before.

"Molly," Jinky said, copying her sister's voice as well as she could, "I know more about dogs than you do, and I say those dogs will protect us. Dogs are always on the side of good people. And what's more they won't hurt your cat, either." It was all settled in Jinky's mind. "What are you going to name your cat?"

While Molly thought for a minute, Jinky broke off a stick from one of the bushes and began making squiggly circles in the loose sand.

If we don't find out he belongs to somebody, and if I get to keep him," Molly said at last, "I'm going to call him Pyewacket. That was the name of a famous cat in a story called *Bell, Book and Candle,* and I—"

"Hey look!" Jinky interrupted. "What's this?" Her stick had hit against something solid buried in the earth. She dropped the stick and began scooping away the sand with both hands.

Molly lifted the kitten to her shoulder and scooted close.

"Maybe it's some of that buried pirate treasure you and Father were talking about," Jinky said excitedly.

But soon she could see it was only a metal plaque which had fallen from a rotted post and been covered by the shifting sands.

Molly blew the plaque clean. Her hair fell over her face as she bent to read aloud:

"A romantic explanation for the name Nags Head is that in the early days of the settlement 'land pirates' deliberately sought to wreck ships. On a stormy night a lantern was tied to the neck of an old nag. The nag was then ridden along the beach. Mistaking the lantern for a beacon . . ."

Molly stopped short and looked up into Jinky's eyes. "Beacon. Lantern. The same words Miss Weatherspoon used."

Jinky nodded.

Molly read on:

> Mistaking the lantern for a beacon, ships were lured to the treacherous reefs, there to be boarded and looted by the wily shoremen.
>
> Legend of Nags Head.

"I don't get it," Jinky said.

Patiently Molly began: "A long time ago—"

"No," Jinky said, "I got that part. I don't understand why Miss Weatherspoon said *I* was mistaking lanterns for beacons."

"She meant something about your saying Mr. McLeod was murdered instead of just plain dying. I'm sure of that. Maybe she thinks of true things as beacons and false things as lanterns. That would make sense. She must have meant that if you didn't quit mistaking lies for the truth you were going to get in trouble."

"I guess so," Jinky agreed, "and we'd better get on home or she'll be madder than she was this morning."

They walked their bikes back onto the highway. Jinky still didn't like Miss Weatherspoon saying she was going to get in trouble. Pete's sake, it was Emmet Saunders who said Mr. McLeod was murdered. All Jinky did was . . . well, she *had* eavesdropped and then repeated what she'd heard. But that wasn't any worse than spying was it? Like that mystery girl . . .

As they rode along, Jinky decided that as soon as they reached home, and put the kitten safely in one of the big packing boxes so he couldn't get out she'd tell Molly about the girl's footprints for sure.

But as it turned out, things were so upset when they got home she did not get a chance to discuss the mystery girl.

They put the kitten in a box and went inside to get him some milk. When they pushed open the swinging door into the kitchen, they found Miss Weatherspoon, still wearing her hat, sitting at the kitchen table sobbing into a man-sized handkerchief.

Jinky and Molly looked at each other in alarm. Miss Weatherspoon had not heard them come in, of course. What could be wrong with her? Finally Jinky pulled together enough courage to tiptoe over and touch Miss Weatherspoon on the shoulder.

The old lady jumped so suddenly that her hat tilted to one side. She looked terribly embarrassed and began to blow her nose loudly into the handkerchief.

"What's wrong?" Jinky cried. Then realizing Miss Weatherspoon would not understand unless she said it more clearly, she shaped the words with her lips: "What is the matter?"

"It's nothing. Nothing at all," Miss Weatherspoon said as she swiped once more at her red nose. Then with a sharp lift of her chin she added, "I reckon this house is just filled with too many ghosts."

"G-ghosts?" Jinky echoed.

A TRIP TO THE ORPHANAGE

"Ghosts?" Molly repeated, looking happier than she had since morning. "Do you really believe in ghosts?"

Miss Weatherspoon gave one last sniffle. Little twinkles replaced some of the sadness in her eyes. "Of course I do! Everyone in Nags Head believes in our own ghost—the ghost of Virginia Dare."

Molly nudged Jinky and tossed her a see-what-did-I-tell-you look.

Jinky glanced from one to the other. "*I* don't believe in ghosts," she blurted. She hoped she had not made Miss Weatherspoon angry again, but somebody around here had to talk sense.

Miss Weatherspoon did seem upset. She looked Jinky in the eye, set her hat straight with both hands, and said tartly, "It's not that a body *believes* in ghosts because there *are* ghosts, but that there *are* ghosts because a body believes in them!"

Molly nodded eagerly to show she understood. But

Jinky thought Miss Weatherspoon was pretty mixed up, and she didn't care if Miss Weatherspoon knew it.

Which she did, because she shook a long finger at Jinky and said, "With my very own eyes I saw the ghost of Virginia Dare one night."

Molly gasped and clapped her hands together. But Jinky's old worry-wart feelings crowded her breathing. And when Molly asked, "What does her ghost look like?" Jinky felt like putting her hands over her ears so she wouldn't hear any more ghost talk. Looks like Molly has made friends with Miss Weatherspoon after all, she thought.

Miss Weatherspoon touched Molly's shoulder. "You can't go pinning ghosts down by insisting on knowing what they look like," she said. "There's lots of things you believe in that you can't say how they look, such as thoughts and plans and dreams and—"

"But," Molly objected, "you said you *saw* her—saw *it,* I mean."

"And I did." Abruptly Miss Weatherspoon turned, sniffed the air, then hobbled toward the stove. For the first time Jinky noticed that spicy smells of cooking filled the room.

"You just let me take a peek at my yam pie," Miss Weatherspoon called over her shoulder, "then I'll set lunch on. While we eat I'll tell you the whole story."

Molly poured a saucer of milk for her kitten. Jinky watched Miss Weatherspoon snatch a straw from the broom, turn the straw upside down, open the oven door, and stick the straw into a velvety-smooth pumpkin-colored pie. Then Miss Weatherspoon pinched her thumb and finger down the straw to see if any raw dough clung to it. "Done to a turn," she pronounced loudly.

In no time at all they were sitting down to tender pink slices of ham, crispy corn pone, and black-eyed peas swimming in thin gravy.

"Now then," Miss Weatherspoon said, whacking both hands on the table top, "I'll tell you the legend of Virginia Dare, and about her ghost that roams these marshes and dunes in the nighttime, and how one moonlit night I saw it for myself."

She picked up the ham platter and passed it to Jinky, who, though she supposed she couldn't help hearing, planned not to believe a single word. Molly, of course, was listening intently.

"When all this started," Miss Weatherspoon began, "only Indians lived here, excepting for a little group of Englishmen who came to find a new home for themselves. Among them was the child Virginia Dare. Nobody rightly knows what caused it, but some terrible, mysterious event happened to these people.

"They disappeared and left no trace behind—no charred houses, no bones, nothing. Soon after they disappeared, the Indians saw this peculiar white doe standing alone and beautiful and sad, facing the sea. Some worried that the doe was a spirit and others declared that it was a good omen."

Miss Weatherspoon buttered some corn pone, laid it down, folded her hands, and went on. "Time and again hunters tried to kill that doe, but it couldn't be done—not with ordinary arrows. That's when the Indians knew for sure this was not an ordinary animal.

"Then one day"—Miss Weatherspoon hesitated, snapped off a bite of her corn pone, chewed and swallowed it—"one day a great hunt was called. One Indian brave, Wanchese was his name, brought along a magic silver arrow. He shot the arrow straight into the doe's heart."

Jinky looked at Molly. Miss Weatherspoon's legend was different than Molly's had been.

Miss Weatherspoon leaned forward and went on. "Wanchese ran up to his victim and right there, as she died, he heard her say the words "Virginia Dare." And under her throat her name was marked clearly in dark hair for all to see! It was then that Nags Head got its ghost. Others have tried to claim her, but she rightly belongs to us."

"How—how do you know this is true?" Jinky asked, since this story was less and less like Molly's. Had Miss Weatherspoon read her legend in a book the way Molly had?

"My own papa told me," Miss Weatherspoon said. "Besides, like I told you, I saw the ghost for myself one night."

Molly's eyes were shining. "Yes?" she breathed.

Jinky forgot about the legends as Miss Weatherspoon began telling what she had seen with her very own eyes.

"Standin' high on a sand dune, over yonder"—
Miss Weatherspoon motioned toward the back yard
—"I've seen many a doe in my life, and this was no
ordinary doe. It was more silvery than white and it
skimmed along gracefully without touchin' a foot to
the ground.

"Right at the top of the dune it stopped running,
floated slowly a few inches down till its paws touched
earth, and stood looking sadly around as if it was
searching for something, or someone. Just then a
cloud passed over the moon. When the cloud moved
on so I could see again, the doe was gone—disappeared
into nowhere, the way it had come."

Molly let out a big sigh. "I wish I could see it some
night. How far was it from here?"

"Just over yonder," Miss Weatherspoon motioned
again. "It was on that highest dune in front of the
land where they've since built the orphanage."

Orphanage! Jinky shot a quick look at Molly, but
Molly still seemed to be deep in the ghost story.
"Miss Weatherspoon," Molly said eagerly, "could you
tell us about another true story that happened here a
long time ago? It's about a murder that is said to have
caused an everlasting bloodstain on the sand."

Miss Weatherspoon frowned, and Molly must have
thought she was trying to remember. "You know,"
Molly went on, "about the long-lost brother who—"

"Long-lost brother? Murder?" Miss Weatherspoon
jumped up so fast she sent her chair clattering to the
floor. "It's all a lie, I tell you. You young'uns been

listening to the tongue-wagging of fools!" The old woman clenched her skinny hands into fists and whacked the table so hard the dishes rattled. "I warned you!" she cried.

Molly stared at Miss Weatherspoon with startled eyes. Jinky felt her own mouth fly open and heard a little choking noise from her throat.

"Who is it keeps telling you about me and my poor brother?" Miss Weatherspoon demanded. "Oh, poor Brother, they'll never stop talking. Even though he's been far away, they never forget."

All at once Miss Weatherspoon's anger seemed to shrivel away and she let her arms fall to her sides. "It's that sorry Emmet Saunders," she moaned, "he's the one can't let folks forget what Brother did."

Jinky's mouth was dry and she tried to swallow, but couldn't. Molly seemed to be so frozen that she couldn't flick an eyelash. She just sat staring at Miss Weatherspoon.

"I didn't reckon on frightening you-all," Miss Weatherspoon said flatly. She picked up the half-empty bowl of peas and clattered toward the counter. "This being the time of year it is, near to bird-hunting time again, and Brother's five years having passed—and being here in this house again makes me edgy. That's what it is. You-all run on out and play."

Miss Weatherspoon looked so miserable that Jinky felt like patting her shoulder and saying everything would be all right. But of course she didn't dare.

Molly whispered, "Come on, Jinky," and Jinky

pushed back her chair and followed Molly through the swinging door.

"Quick," Molly urged as soon as they were out of Miss Weatherspoon's sight. "Let's get out of this house. She's crazy! I know she is. *She* thinks that story was about *her* brother. But the bloodstain on the sand and the long-lost brother story happened hundreds of years ago. Maybe she believes in reincarnation or something. You heard her, Jinky, she said that old legend was really about her and her brother."

"Crazy?" Jinky caught Molly's hand as they ran out the front door. "Oh, Molly, what are we going to do? Even the dogs . . ." Jinky fought to keep from crying. It wouldn't do a bit of good and would only make Molly feel worse. "We'll think of something," she declared as they stopped on the porch for breath. "Let's hide. I know a good place. Down there behind the statue of—"

Jinky squeezed Molly's hand. "Look!"

Both girls stared in amazement as the figure of a girl in blue jeans, with shirttail flying, darted from behind the Virginia Dare statue. The girl skimmed across the driveway, crossed the moat bridge, and disappeared behind the thick bushes on the far side.

"Molly, it's her!"

"Who?"

"The mystery girl. She's been spying on us, only I never got the chance to tell. Twice I've seen them— footprints. Back there where she came from just now. Hurry. Let's see where she went."

But by the time the twins got across the bridge, the girl was disappearing around the edge of a distant dune.

"Her house must be back there someplace," Molly said.

Jinky dropped Molly's hand. She chewed thoughtfully at a rough spot on her lip. "Molly, did that girl look like somebody you know?"

"She looked like . . . She looked about our age, and . . ." Molly rolled her eyes toward Jinky. She looked at Jinky as if she were seeing her for the first time. For a second she just stared. Then she dug her fingers into Jinky's arm. "She's the one! She must be Lily Joe. The one Miss Weatherspoon back in town thought was you! *She looks that much like you.*"

"And the orphanage where she lives—where the other Miss Weatherspoon said they don't allow cats —is the one our Miss Weatherspoon said was back there. Jinky pointed toward the dune far across the flat stretch of land.

Molly frowned. "Why did she run? Everyone in this town acts crazy." She shivered as she looked back toward their house.

"I know what," Jinky said. "Why don't we follow that girl and ask her about Miss Weatherspoon? We know she knows her, because the other Weatherspoon sister talked as if Lily Joe came to their house real often. We could find out if Miss Weatherspoon is crazy or not—and find out what kind of hospital she has."

"And what will we do," Molly demanded, "if we find out Miss Weatherspoon *is* crazy?"

"Then we'll call the folks," Jinky answered, and both girls nodded to seal the bargain.

As Molly and Jinky started down along the row of yaupon bushes, the dogs bounded up to them. "Hey, good, the dogs are coming, too," Molly surprised Jinky by saying. Jinky noticed that Molly even gingerly put a hand out toward Duke, who was the more friendly of the two.

But the dogs stopped at the edge of a patch of feathery-leafed sea oat and no amount of coaxing would make them go a step farther. "They've probably been trained to stop at our property line," Molly said as Jinky gave up calling to them.

The girls hurried past clumps of bright-colored wildflowers that looked as if they'd been picked and stuck into the sand. By the time they reached the dune where the strange girl had disappeared, the early afternoon sky had turned greenish-gray.

The wind had died down completely. When Jinky looked back toward their house, she noticed that a faint fog was gathering again over the ocean. She thought about darkness coming and being alone in the house with Miss Weatherspoon. "Let's run," she urged, starting up the side of the sand dune.

Even before they reached the top, they saw the orphanage. "It's awfully big to *live* in," Jinky said, stopping a moment to get a good look. The orphanage, set back from a narrow road, was a three-story building made of red brick.

As they drew nearer, they saw that the high iron fence around the building had a gate.

The yard, unlike most other yards they'd seen in Nags Head, had grass growing in it. Halfway up to the building there was a sign that said KEEP OFF THE GRASS.

"But it doesn't say No Trespassing," Jinky said, opening the gate.

There was no one in sight, but they could hear shouts and laughter from the back of the building. "I've never seen an orphanage before," Jinky told Molly as they inched cautiously up the wide walk.

"I have, in books," Molly replied. "Look, above the door, 'Sunshine Home.' That's a nice name for one."

Sunshine Home—the name on Father's card, Jinky thought. Why did Father have that card? Could this orphanage have something to do with the secret?

Jinky's mind spun with questions, but there was no time to discuss them with Molly, because they were already cutting across the grass, tiptoeing quietly and carefully, on account of the sign, toward the direction of the voices.

Side by side, Molly and Jinky edged toward the end of the building. By the far wall two boys, who looked about their own age, were climbing an iron fire escape that wound up to a pair of windows on the second floor. The twins stopped short, but though the boys stared down they didn't speak.

Jinky gave Molly a little push and they went on past the boys until they could see the back yard, which turned out to be an enormous playground. It was even bigger than the schoolyard back home.

At first glance it looked like there were a million children swarming over the large area. Jinky was staring so hard she almost bumped into a tall "giant-stride" with its hand bars tangled together as if the last children to swing around on it had twisted the long chains over and under in a Maypole game.

Not far from the deserted giant-stride a group of very small children were splashing in some water around a faucet on a pipe sticking out of the ground. The little ones were squealing and stomping mud on each other. They paid no attention to Jinky and Molly.

Jinky saw some boys playing one-o-cat on a marked-off ball diamond. Toward the center of the yard, under a big tree, a man was helping some children put up a tire swing.

Suddenly a girl dropped down out of the tree. She started running toward the little children at the spigot. It was the mystery girl!

The girl didn't see Jinky and Molly at first. She seemed to be concerned about one of the children. "Abbey, you get yourself out of that—" Then she saw the twins and stopped.

There was no doubt that this mystery girl was also the Lily Joe the "other" Miss Weatherspoon mistook Jinky for. She was a tiny bit taller than Jinky, and her hair was a shade darker, but otherwise they could have been identical twins!

Jinky looked the girl over from head to toe. Yes,

she was even wearing a pair of very worn sneakers. Jinky had the spooky feeling that she was looking at herself in a mirror—herself with an unpleasant look on her face. She almost knew what the girl was going to say as she watched her swagger closer as if she intended to challenge them to a fight.

"You-all better get out of here."

"Aren't visitors allowed?" Molly asked primly.

"Visitors are. Snoopers ain't!"

Jinky couldn't help thinking that she and Molly weren't being nearly as snoopy as this girl herself had been ever since they'd moved into the Yaupon Moat house. But she didn't say so.

The girl narrowed her eyes. "And you can tell your pa not to come snoopin' around here no more neither."

"Our father does not snoop!" Molly cried.

"Then keep him offen this property. We don't have no truck with comers 'n' goers like you-all."

Molly drew herself up. "We only came here to ask you a civilized question."

The girl's sudden grin was more like a jeer. "Ask me no questions, and I'll tell you no lies," she recited, the same as Miss Weatherspoon had earlier.

"When people meet," Molly said, tossing her long hair, "it's polite to introduce themselves. I'm Molly Smith. This is my twin sister, Jinky Smith."

"Twins! Ha!" Lily Joe snorted. "I reckon her and me look more like twins than you-all do." Then she spit on the ground as if to show how bad it was to look like Jinky.

"Many people," Molly said in the tone of voice she used with people much younger than she was, "many people have a look-alike someplace in the world. My father says so. Tell us your name."

"I ain't got no name, Miss Prissy," the orphan girl replied and turned rudely away. "Look at you, Abbey," she said, pulling the little girl from the puddle.

Jinky couldn't help noticing how much softer and nicer the girl's voice became when she spoke to the child. She watched Lily Joe kneel down and begin scrubbing at the mud on the smaller girl's legs with her own shirttail.

The little girl had a round babyish face and beautifully brushed curls. Her eyes were sparkling and happy even while she was being scolded.

"Mud all up your legs!" Lily Joe muttered.

Jinky saw that in spite of the girl's grumbly words her hand was gentle as she rubbed. Then Jinky glanced up because, out of the corner of her eye, she caught sight of the man approaching who had been helping with the swing.

No one else had noticed him yet. Certainly not Lily Joe, who had her back to him. "I don't want you-all havin' no truck with Abbey here, either," she cried, squinting up at the twins. "G'wan! Scat! Git!"

"Hold on there, Lily Joe!" the man's voice boomed out behind Lily Joe, and she jumped like a scared frog. But she pulled Abbey closer and scowled at the man sullenly.

The man spoke much more kindly than Jinky expected him to, considering the way Lily Joe was act-ing. "Why don't you introduce me to your friends?"

"They ain't no friends of mine."

"Lily Joe, do you know these girls' names or don't you?"

Abbey began tugging to get free from Lily Joe's hand. She looked longingly toward the other small children, who were still splashing.

Lily Joe let go of the child's hand without seeming to realize she had, and the child went straight back to the puddle.

"Lily Joe!" The man's voice was stern this time.

Lily Joe scuffed sand toward Molly. "That there one is named Molly and the other'n Jinky. Their last name's Smith, but knowin' their names don't make them my friends."

The man ignored that remark. "Now I think it would be nice of you, Lily Joe, to show these girls around our home."

When Lily Joe didn't move or answer but just kept kicking at the sand, the man said, "Right now, you hear!"

"Okay, okay," Lily Joe grumbled. "I reckon they can wait long enough for me to get Abbey." She turned and gently pulled the child back out of the water, paying no attention that the chubby legs were even muddier than before.

Lily Joe, holding Abbey's hand, started off across the playground, and, though it seemed awkward, Jinky and Molly followed along.

Jinky tried to think of something to say that would sound friendly. "Is Abbey your sister?" she asked.

Lily Joe didn't turn around. "She's my keep-sister," she said in a bored voice.

"What's a keep-sister?" Jinky asked, wondering if Molly already knew.

Lily Joe gave a big sigh. "A keep-sister is just what it says—a sister you keep, keep care of, read stories to, give baths to. The boys have keep-brothers, girls have keep-sisters. Anything else you want to know, go read a book."

Lily Joe looked down at the pretty child. Her voice changed suddenly as she said, "All the girls wanted you, didn't they, Abbey? Because you're the cutest and have curly hair. But I got you."

The little girl beamed up at Lily Joe, who smiled back. Jinky couldn't help noticing how much better Lily Joe looked when she smiled.

Jinky wondered if Lily Joe really hated her and Molly, or if she was just pretending to for some reason. But why? And why did she say that about Father snooping around here. He *could* have been here. He *did* have that card.

They had reached the back door now, and the twins followed Lily Joe into a huge kitchen. It smelled of gingerbread and hot soapsuds. Two ladies in white uniforms were buttering stacks of sliced bread. None of the girls spoke as they marched straight through the kitchen and into the dining room. This room was filled with long tables covered with white oilcloth.

Without a word Lily Joe led the way up a narrow back stairway.

Jinky noticed that the rubber mats on the steps were worn clear through in the middle. The steps led up to a wide hall. Molly stopped in front of a bronze wall-plaque. Lily Joe waited with raised eyebrows and hands on hips while Molly read aloud,

> This institution has received funds from the H. P. McLeod trust, established by his widow, Vera Telling McLeod."

Watching Lily Joe's face as Molly read, Jinky thought again that she could almost tell what Lily Joe would say next.

Sure enough! "We can read for ourselves," Lily Joe muttered and stomped on down the hall. She stopped at the door second from the end.

"I reckon you're curious to see what a bedroom looks like," she said, making a mock bow and standing aside to let them through the door. "Feast your eyes."

There were four beds in the large room, one in each corner. Each bed had a different-colored spread, which Jinky thought made the room very pretty. The windows, overlooking the playground, were wide open, and a breeze puffed the long curtains. Jinky thought it looked like a cozy place to sleep.

There was one dresser in the room. Across the top of it was a long, narrow scarf neatly embroidered in flower patterns. Beside the dresser hung a metal tooth-

brush holder with four blue toothbrushes. Jinky wondered how they told them apart until she saw that
each one had a tape around its handle with a name
inked on it.

"It's nice!" Jinky said, and she meant it. It would
be fun sharing a room with so many people.

"You can sit on my bed if you want," Lily Joe said
in the kindest voice she had used since she met them.

Immediately little Abbey began to shout, "I want
to sit on your bed, too."

"No," Lily Joe said firmly, "you'd bounce on it."
But she pulled the child down onto the linoleum rug
beside her and began to tickle her playfully. Abbey
swung a small fist, which Lily Joe dodged as she
pulled a pitcher's glove out from under the bed. Lily
Joe plopped her fist into the groove of the glove, and
Jinky could almost feel the buttery smoothness of the
leather herself.

"I'm the best pitcher around here," Lily Joe
bragged.

"Counting boys?" Jinky asked.

"Counting everyone. Even the supe."

"You mean your superintendent?" Molly asked.
"Jinky is a good baseball player, too."

"Nobody pitches good as me!" Lily Joe said.

"As well as I," Molly corrected.

Lily Joe's face turned red, and Jinky tried to think
of some way to change the subject. "What we wanted
to ask you," she said hurriedly, "was about Miss
Weatherspoon."

"What of her?" Lily Joe's face had that suspicious look again.

"Is she—" Jinky was afraid Lily Joe would laugh if she used the word crazy. "Is she . . . nice?" she finished lamely.

Lily Joe snickered. "She's stayin' with you, ain't she?"

"Isn't she," Molly said.

Lily Joe stuck her tongue out at Molly. "No, she ain't nice. She's mean and wicked and probably plannin' to cut out your gizzard in the night when you-all are asleep."

"That's a lie!" Molly cried, and Jinky could see Molly was trying to hide how scared she was.

"It ain't no blasted lie neither. And besides that, her brother is a murderer and he's due to come back. He'll probably murder you-all, too, 'less she gets around to it first."

Abbey began to whimper, and Lily Joe cuddled her onto her lap. She turned so their backs were to the twins and began rocking herself back and forth.

Molly grabbed Jinky's hand and pulled her to her feet and toward the door. Jinky looked back and caught a glimpse of Lily Joe's face. It was crumpled with a mixture of anger and hate and something else —fear? What was she scared of?

Molly hurried them along so fast that the girls missed the back stairway, but they found a front stairs. It was wider than the one they'd come up, with shiny banisters and red figured carpeting. They dashed down the stairs.

While they were still tugging at the knob of the heavy front door, Lily Joe appeared at the head of the steps. "And don't you-all never come snoopin' round again, ya hear?"

Jinky was sure she heard a sob just before the door swung shut behind them.

TROUBLE AT SUNSHINE HOME

When Jinky and Molly were halfway to the gate, Molly put her arm out to slow Jinky to a walk. "Let's not give Lily Joe the satisfaction of thinking she scared us away," Molly said. "She's the most hateful girl I ever met in my whole life."

Jinky glanced back over her shoulder. "I feel kind of sorry for her."

"Ha!" Molly planted one heel after another firmly on the front walk. "I don't."

As they hurried through the gate, Jinky noticed uneasily that the greenish sky had darkened to charcoal color. Behind the big dune in the distance black clouds hung heavy and low. "Do you think she was lying about Miss Weatherspoon?" Jinky asked.

"Of course. You heard all those other lies she told about our father snooping around the orphanage. Ha!"

"But that part wasn't a lie . . . I don't think."

Jinky didn't know why she defended the orphan girl,
unless it was because she wished Molly hadn't acted
so uppity about the way Lily Joe talked.

"What do you mean, that wasn't a lie?" Molly demanded, snatching off a stalk of stiff grass and break-
ing it to bits as she walked along.

"Father could have gone there back when he rented
our house," Jinky explained, "because this morning,
before the folks left, when I carried his things to him,
I saw a card that had 'Sunshine Home' printed on it."

Molly stopped and faced Jinky. "Honest?"

"And I could tell by the way the folks looked at
each other that card was important."

They walked along in silence. Jinky stole a glance
at Molly's face, and she could almost see the thinking
wheels going around in her head. There was a rumble
of far-off thunder, and Jinky shivered. She supposed
Molly was thinking about those awful boxes marked
"heads" and "bodies," and the way Miss Weatherspoon acted every time someone mentioned the word
murder, and about how mixed-up Miss Weatherspoon was about the legend of the bloodstained
sand.

Jinky wished they had at least asked Lily Joe about
the hospital. What would they do when they got back
to the house where Miss Weatherspoon was waiting
for them?

They had passed the row of dunes and were almost
to the darkening cluster of yaupon bushes when
Jinky said, "I'm practically sure Lily Joe was lying

about Miss Weatherspoon." But even as she said it, she heard the questioning sound in her own voice.

When Molly said nothing but kept marching straight ahead, Jinky added, "I *know* she was lying, because I could tell how she felt inside. You know— like with somebody you've known a long time."

Molly's eyes narrowed and her lips drew tight. "Like she really was your twin, you mean?"

"Yes," Jinky said and instantly wished she hadn't. "No!" she cried, feeling confused.

Molly drew herself up. "It doesn't matter what you felt. And it doesn't matter to *me* whether Lily Joe was lying about Miss Weatherspoon or not."

This surprised Jinky. Now it was her turn to put her arm out and stop Molly. "Why not?"

"Because I have everything all figured out and *I* might as well be dead!"

Jinky gasped. She knew Molly liked to make things as dramatic and exciting as possible, but Molly had never said anything like— *What* did Molly have figured out? Jinky was almost afraid to ask.

She was afraid because way back in her mind she was beginning to piece things together herself. It started with the way she and Lily Joe looked so much alike. Then the talk about the mysterious "she" Father saw when he came here the first time, and what Mother said yesterday about "things that were so important they change everyone's lives. "Molly," she began warily.

"Jinky Smith, you saw that girl the same as I did.

You saw how much alike you two are. *She is your very own twin.* Which means, of course, that I'm not! There *was* a mix-up when we were born, after all."

"But that's impossible!" Jinky's nose suddenly itched like she was going to burst into tears.

"It is *not* impossible. Even that moving man said it happens every day."

They had reached the edge of the bridge now, and Molly stopped as if she never intended to go another step. "I don't know if you realize it or not, Jinky, but when we were born our country was at war with both Japan and Germany. Things got mixed up every day. Father was overseas. He was in that prisoner of war camp, so he couldn't look out for us. Mother came here to Nags Head, where she didn't know a person except Grandmother Smith. All the reliable doctors and nurses were probably away helping the soldiers. Somebody unreliable put the babies in the wrong cribs!"

Molly seemed so sure. "What are we going to *do?*" Jinky cried.

Molly turned away, her shoulders stiff. "You mean what am *I* going to do? You are going to stay right here and live with the folks like you always have—*and* with Lily Joe. I'm going to run away."

"Molly, you can't. Don't. Why would you?"

"I'm not going to be stuck in that old orphanage."

Jinky was really crying now. "But the folks would never put—"

"Jinky"—Molly whirled to face her—"they may

not have anything to say about it. There are laws, you know, or maybe you don't. I'm sure the folks *tried* to keep me. But they failed and that's why they moved here to Nags Head instead of just adopting Lily Joe and bringing her to Centerville to live with us. Mother told us that she and Father worked very hard to make everything about the secret come out right, because it was going to affect all our lives. Don't you see, moving here to stay close to me is the best they can do."

Jinky suddenly thought of something. "Then why did Mother say they'd need my help more than yours?"

"I never did believe *that!*"

"But she *did*."

"Well, *if* she did, she said it because she knows you're a worry-wart, and I'm not. She knows that even if I am an orphan, I can take care of myself."

Jinky was speechless. She shook her head while salty tears ran into the corners of her mouth. "B-but what about the detective?" she sobbed. "Why did they hire that detective from England?"

"I don't know," Molly said. "Maybe my real parents came here from England the same as Virginia Dare's did long ago. That part doesn't matter. What matters is that I'm going to disappear the same as Virginia Dare did—right now, before the folks get back to stop me." Molly turned away and began walking fast toward the house.

"Stop!" Jinky ran after her. "You can't leave me here alone. Where will you go?"

"I'll go down to one of the piers and stow away on a boat. My cat and me—like Dick Whittington in the story."

She's brave enough to do it, too! Jinky thought in a panic. "What will Father say?" she called after Molly. "Think how awful they'll feel."

"What do I care?" Molly flung back. "I'm not their child."

Desperately, Jinky tried to think of something she could promise Molly if only she would stay.

"I'll steal you a hundred new petticoats if you won't run away," she pleaded.

"Don't you dare steal, Jinky, not ever." Molly turned back and put her arm around Jinky's waist. "Oh, Jinky, when I'm far away in some foreign country I'll worry about you so. You eavesdrop and lie something awful, and you'll learn to talk like that horrid girl, and I'll never know if Miss Weatherspoon —" Molly dropped her arms to her sides. "Maybe I'll stay till the folks get back," she said with a sigh. "But not one minute after. While they are unpacking, I'll slip away. No one here will ever see me again as long as they live—not even you. Jinky, if I stay till they come, promise you won't tell them I'm leaving."

Jinky would have promised anything. She felt the stone that her heart had become soften a little. "I promise," she agreed. But I'll think of some way to stop her, she vowed to herself. She felt so obliged to Molly for not leaving right then that she wanted to do something wonderful for her—make her feel happier somehow. "Molly," she said, "you go see how Pyewacket is doing. I'll go inside, and I'll just walk right up to that crazy Miss Weatherspoon, and I'll *ask* her what kind of a hospital she has in her house." Even facing a dragon would be easy now, after facing losing Molly.

Jinky wanted so much to do something for Molly that she could have hugged Molly when she agreed. She started up the porch steps, but turned. "You won't run away while I'm gone, will you?"

"I won't," Molly promised.

On the way inside Jinky thought about how good it was that she could count on Molly to keep her word. If only this gets settled somehow, she vowed, I am going to learn to be as honest as Molly is.

Jinky found Miss Weatherspoon in the kitchen working over the sink. She was not surprised this time to see the wide-brimmed hat still on her head.

But before Jinky got the courage to ask her question, Miss Weatherspoon bobbed over, put both hands on Jinky's shoulders, and said, "Will you phone up Sister for me and ask her if Brother has come home yet?"

Why doesn't *she* do it? Jinky wondered uneasily. Then she remembered that since Miss Weatherspoon couldn't hear, she couldn't use the telephone. That must have been the reason Mother thought her voice sounded different the day she called her. It must have been the other Miss Weatherspoon doing the talking.

Reluctantly, Jinky nodded that she would make the call.

"The number is 8076," Miss Weatherspoon said.

"Oh, I do hope she says yes." She clasped her bony hands together and looked up as if she were praying.

Jinky couldn't help praying the answer would be no, after what Lily Joe said about Brother being a murderer.

And it was. Jinky repeated the other Miss Weatherspoon's message distinctly, word for word. "Tell Sister not to worry, though. His time is up and he'll come home today."

Time up? Jinky wondered miserably. She thought of Lily Joe's threatening words, "He's a murderer and will probably come back and . . ." Had Brother been in *prison?*

Jinky shivered as she stared at Miss Weatherspoon's crumpled-looking face. I can't possibly ask about her hospital now, she thought. Jinky turned quickly away, wondering what she should tell Molly.

I could tell her I asked, she thought, and that she said it was nothing but a rest home for old people. But Jinky's plans were sharply interrupted by the shrill ring of the phone.

The unexpected sound made Jinky jump, but Miss Weatherspoon didn't even look up.

Jinky reached slowly for the receiver. Would it be Sister again, saying Brother had come, after all?

Jinky's spirits shot up when she recognized Mother's voice.

"It's me. It's Jinky," she answered back. First she asked about Father, planning next to tell Mother about the terrible mess they were in.

"He's much better," Mother said happily, which

made Jinky feel happy, too, in spite of everything.

"That's why I called," Mother went on. "So you girls wouldn't worry. And to see how you are getting along."

Now was Jinky's chance. She glanced at Miss Weatherspoon. No need to worry about her overhearing. But Mother sounded so far away, and so gay, almost like she was off on a trip having fun. I can't do it, Jinky decided. I can't worry her now. "We're fine," she said. "Molly found a new cat, can she keep him?"

"We'll see," Mother answered. "I guess it would be all right. Now you tell Miss Weatherspoon we'll be home late tomorrow afternoon. Father has his last appointment at four. Goodbye, dear. Give Molly my love."

Late tomorrow. Jinky held on to the receiver until she heard the final far-off click. It was as though a key had turned in a lock, shutting her out.

What would Molly say about her telling Mother they were fine? Too late she realized she could have at least asked Mother if she knew about Miss Weatherspoon's hospital. *That* wouldn't have worried Mother. Jinky sighed. I was too dumb to think of it. Molly would have.

Anyway, she could tell Molly that Father was better, and that Molly could keep the kitten. But then she remembered Molly wouldn't be here long, and she'd be taking the kitten with her. Jinky pushed through the door feeling as gloomy as Miss Weatherspoon looked.

In spite of her being an orphan now, Molly did smile a little when she heard Father was better. She didn't say a word when Jinky told her about the call to the other Miss Weatherspoon and only shrugged when Jinky asked, "Do you think their brother has been in prison?"

When Jinky told Molly she'd been afraid to ask Miss Weatherspoon about the hospital, Molly only said, "It doesn't matter." She acted as if she had more important things on her mind now than being afraid of an old lady.

Jinky felt terribly alone and sad. Never had she loved Molly so much, or admired her more. She pictured how *she* would feel if there was another girl who looked like Molly's twin. But she wiped that picture out of her mind, because she knew she'd act even worse if there were such a girl.

Molly was quiet all through supper and while they were bedding down her cat in his box. Jinky decided she would have to take over protecting both herself and Molly for the night. So as soon as Miss Weatherspoon was busy in another part of the house, Jinky quietly coaxed the dogs inside. They walked stiff-legged and slow on the polish floors, but she finally got them up the steps and into her bedroom without getting caught.

Molly hardly seemed to notice the dogs. "I guess I'll read in bed awhile," she said listlessly and picked up *The Secret Garden*.

Jinky saw that the window was open and decided to close it. For a minute she watched the mist rolling in from the swamps over toward town. A three-quarter moon sailed high in the sky, and Jinky realized the clouds of this afternoon had blown over without the threatened storm.

She blinked as Baron growled low in his throat behind her. Had he heard a noise outside? She looked down to where the giant oaks loomed through the vapors like hulks of old ships. The tree leaves, silvered by moonlight, looked like ghostly masts. Jinky heard no sound except the frogs and the splashing of water in the moat.

Then suddenly something moved beside one of the far trees. She strained to see through the curling fog. Her scalp prickled and she caught her breath sharply. It was a man!

The dogs! What a terrible mistake it had been to bring the dogs inside. If they were out there now, they'd chase that prowler away.

Jinky watched, too scared to move, as the man crept noiselessly toward the house. His shoulders slouched forward, his hair was blond—no, gray. Not until he was almost under the window could Jinky manage to lift her arms and slam the window down.

She ran to Molly's bed. "There's a man trying to get in this house!" she whispered hoarsely.

"You're trying to get me to stop reading."

"No, honest."

Molly dropped her book. "Are you sure?"

Jinky nodded. She tried to stop her chattering teeth. "We'd better find Miss Weatherspoon."

With trembling fingers they flung on their robes and pushed their feet into slippers. Clasping hands, they tiptoed cautiously along the hall and down the steps. Thank goodness Molly didn't run away and leave me here alone, Jinky thought and gave her sister's hand an extra squeeze.

Miss Weatherspoon was not in the living room. They crept toward the kitchen. But even before they reached the door, they heard voices. They stopped and looked at each other with terrified eyes. Had the prowler broken in already? Was he holding Miss Weatherspoon prisoner right now in the kitchen?

They had to find out! They moved like two shadows toward the door. Gingerly, Jinky put out her shaking hand and edged the door inward a fraction of an inch. She put one eye to the crack. Her other hand flew to her mouth. It was all she could do to keep from screaming. That man—the one she had seen stealing up to the house—was towering over poor Miss Weatherspoon, who was fanning her face with a hot pad holder.

BAD NEWS FOR MOLLY

Jinky motioned frantically for Molly to look. Molly peeped through the crack, then grabbed Jinky with an icy hand.

Jinky eased the door shut. "Let's get help."

"How?" Molly whispered back. "The phone's—" She pointed toward the kitchen.

We can't leave Miss Weatherspoon trapped like that, Jinky thought desperately. "The dogs!" She shaped the words silently. "Let's get the—"

But Molly, who had again opened the door a crack, beckoned Jinky to look.

Jinky peeked over Molly's shoulder. Now Miss Weatherspoon was pouring the stranger a cup of coffee! And after she put it in front of him, she laid her hand on his shoulder—which she would never do if he were holding her captive.

With a bouncy flip of her hat, Miss Weatherspoon sat down across from the man. "I'm rightly glad," she said, "that you came over here soon as you'd seen Sister, even if this house does—But land sakes, all these years!"

The man ran his fingers through his thick hair. "I wanted to let you-all know where I was, but—"

"Now, Charles"—Miss Weatherspoon patted his arm—"you put your mind to something else this very minute. You know what Papa always told us about mistaking lanterns for beacons."

Jinky and Molly stared at each other in stunned silence. This man was the brother of the two Miss Weatherspoons—the brother Lily Joe said was a murderer! A *murderer* right here in this house!

Just then Jinky heard a faint clicking sound coming from the hall behind her. She glanced back and saw that Duke had followed them downstairs.

Duke stopped, cocked his head, and gave a little questioning bark.

"Sh-h-h." Jinky put her finger to her lips and looked anxiously at the kitchen door. Miss Weatherspoon wouldn't hear, but her brother—

Her brother had heard! The kitchen door swung wide, almost sweeping Jinky and Molly off their feet. Both girls screamed.

Charles Weatherspoon stared down at them. His arms hung at his sides. He frowned in a puzzled way as if he couldn't think what to say or do.

Then Miss Weatherspoon saw the girls and hopped out of her chair. She hurried over to where they stood. "Land sakes!" she exclaimed. "You two look pale as ghosts. This is Brother. He's come home like I said he would."

Jinky backed off a step. She could tell by the way Miss Weatherspoon's sharp eyes searched their faces that the old lady knew they were scared. "We . . . we . . ." she began, but couldn't go on. She looked to Molly for help. But Molly's eyes were wide with fear and *she* was chewing a fingernail, Pete's sake! Poohw raw, Jinky thought wildly, but this time it did no good.

"Well I declare," Miss Weatherspoon said. "I do believe it's those stories you heard—those stories that were nothing but sorry old lanterns! You mistook them for beacons. You two come out here and sit. I'll tell you the honest story. You sit too, Charles."

Reluctantly, Jinky and Molly followed Miss Weatherspoon and her brother into the brightly lit kitchen. Everything that was happening seemed unreal as a dream to Jinky. She saw Duke settle himself on the floor beside Charles Weatherspoon and felt a little better. Surely Duke, who was being gentle as a lamb, wouldn't act this way around a murderer.

"It was five years ago today," Miss Weatherspoon began with a flap of her hat brim. "Charles here was hunting. It was goose season. Con—that was Mr. McLeod's first name—had just finished building this house. We were all good friends. He invited Charles to come hunt on his land.

"Brother didn't know it, but Mr. McLeod was back yonder by the edge of the moat. It was still called Drowning Creek then. Brother was far down the other side, behind that big clump of yaupon bushes by the bridge."

Miss Weatherspoon patted her brother's arm again. He gave her a crooked smile and nodded his head for her to go on.

"Brother tripped," Miss Weatherspoon said. "His gun went off accidently." The old lady stopped talking, and Jinky saw one little tear running down her wrinkled cheek.

Then Miss Weatherspoon sniffed and lifted her chin. "The shot hit Con McLeod—barely grazed his scalp, but he fell, unconscious. His face was in the water. He was not found in time. He drowned. It was a terrible accident, but no one's to blame, least of all Charles." For the first time since she came to this house, Jinky saw that Miss Weatherspoon had a smile on her face as she finished up. "Now you two jump off to bed, you hear?"

As soon as Jinky and Molly were back in their beds, with Duke settled in the corner by the door, they began whispering excitedly.

"Pete's sake," Jinky said, "Miss Weatherspoon isn't crazy after all."

"Right," Molly agreed. "No wonder she thought I was talking about her and her brother when I asked about the bloodstains on the sand."

Jinky wiggled her toes. "And that accident must have been the tragedy that came between Mrs. McLeod and Miss Weatherspoon. And it's why Miss Weatherspoon said this house was filled with ghosts out of the past. And it is also probably the reason Mrs. McLeod didn't want Yaupon Moat called Drowning Creek any more."

"And," Molly said, whacking her pillow with both fists, "it means that Lily Joe was *lying* about Miss Weatherspoon's brother Charles being a murderer." Molly put her cheek down on the pillow. "She's an untruthful girl, Jinky, and I'm sorry she's your hon-est-to-goodness twin. Good night." Molly sighed deeply and closed her eyes.

Jinky had been hoping Molly had forgotten about Lily Joe—at least for the time being. She listened as Molly drew a long breath almost like a sob. Poor Molly, she thought, what could I promise her that would make things better?

"Molly," she whispered with a sudden idea, "the very first thing in the morning I'll go back to that or-phanage and ask Lily Joe where she was born. If she wasn't born here in Nags Head, where we were born, then there couldn't have been a mix-up. But," she added quickly, "you have to promise not to run away while I'm gone."

"I promise," Molly said in a little trailing-off voice, then louder, "but I might leave as soon as you get back —if she *was* born here."

Jinky crossed her fingers under her covers and wished that Lily Joe was born in Kalamazoo or any-where but Nags Head. She felt so sorry for Molly that she was even glad when Molly went to sleep first. She thought about Miss Weatherspoon and her brother downstairs, and about how different things seem when you know the honest story. Pete's sake, tomorrow sure, she'd simply ask Miss Weatherspoon what was in those boxes marked "heads" and "bodies."

Jinky watched the pendulum and weights wag peacefully beneath the wall clock. Both dogs were snoring now. In spite of the importance of what she would find out at the orphanage tomorrow morning, she sort of looked forward to seeing Lily Joe again. She wondered if Lily Joe really could pitch better than anyone around here.

Would Lily Joe be mad because she came back? If only Lily Joe knew where she was born, and if only it was someplace besides this town, Jinky decided she didn't care how cross Lily Joe was.

As Jinky drifted off to sleep, she planned exactly what she would say to Lily Joe. She closed her eyes, and when she woke suddenly it was early morning and she'd been having a bad dream.

Molly wasn't awake yet, but the dogs were watching Jinky expectantly. Trying to shake the dream from her mind, Jinky hurried around looking for a clean sweatshirt and jeans. She was as quiet as possible, hoping Molly wouldn't wake up.

But all the time Jinky was skinning into her clothes the bad dream she'd had clung like witch's moss to her mind. In the dream Jinky had seen the ghost of Virginia Dare outside her window in a swirling fog. The ghost was crying, pleading to be let in. Now as Jinky thought about the shadowy dream face, she realized it had looked exactly like Molly's.

She brushed hard at her hair, trying to push the

dream out of her head. When she finished brushing, she whispered to Duke and Baron, "Come on, fellas."

Halfway down the steps Jinky heard the clatter of pans from the kitchen and knew Miss Weatherspoon was already up. She let Duke and Baron out the front door, wondering if Miss Weatherspoon would still be wearing her hat this morning.

Sure enough, Miss Weatherspoon was sitting at the round table snapping beans and humming off-key while the faded velvet roses kept time.

Miss Weatherspoon hopped up cheerfully when she saw Jinky. She took a warm plate from the oven. Jinky looked at the grits and eggs, the tiny crisps of fried potatoes, and thought she'd never been so hungry. She smiled Miss Weatherspoon a good-morning and thank-you all in one.

As soon as she finished eating, Jinky rinsed her plate, then faced Miss Weatherspoon. "Tell Molly I've gone on that walk we talked about," she said distinctly.

"Don't go too far. There's a mackerel sky," Miss Weatherspoon warned.

Jinky wondered how far too far was, and what a mackerel sky meant, but decided it was better not to ask.

The gray moss on the trees still sparkled from last night's fog, but once Jinky left the tree-shaded yard behind, a misty-yellow heat moved with her across the dune-dotted land.

As she passed the tallest dune, a large bird flapped its wings lazily above the feathered stalks of sea oat.

Except for the bird's flapping wings it was very quiet. To Jinky the walk seemed shorter than it had the day before.

She reached the orphanage playground, where a few children were sitting in the sun talking, but Lily Joe wasn't one of them.

Then Jinky saw her. Lily Joe was standing alone on the pitcher's mound of the ball diamond. Jinky stopped beside the giant-stride and watched her look-alike, who was listlessly swinging a baseball bat at the empty air.

She wondered if Lily Joe would chase her away if she went out to the mound. She held her back stiff and walked toward the gunny sack that marked home plate.

"Thought I told you to keep offen this property," Lily Joe yelled before Jinky was two steps off home plate.

Jinky drew a sharp breath. "You've been coming on our property whenever you pleased," she yelled right back.

Lily Joe's eyebrows shot up and a flicker of admiration crossed her face. This gave Jinky the courage to go nearer.

To her surprise she saw that the orphan girl's eyes were red-rimmed and swollen, and the tip of her nose was pink, the same as Jinky's always was when she cried a long time.

"What's wrong?" Jinky asked bluntly.

Lily Joe hunched her right shoulder high and

swung the bat hard. "Nothin'!" she said. "None of your business."

There was an awkward silence while Jinky stood there wondering what to do next. It would sound dumb, she decided, to blurt out, "Where were you born?" She watched Lily Joe swing the bat one time after another as if she were alone again.

The silence got worse, and Jinky was about to say anything that popped into her mind, when she was startled to feel something grab her hand. She looked down. It was Abbey, Lily Joe's keep-sister.

"Hey"—Abbey smiled up at Jinky as if they were old friends—"you look just like my Joey, and do you know what? I might get 'dopted."

Lily Joe dropped her bat, grabbed Abbey, and clapped her hand over her mouth. "You little dumb-bell. You're not neither going to get adopted. Go on away and play."

But the second Lily Joe uncovered Abbey's mouth the child yelled, "Joey, do I want to get 'dopted?"

"Maybe you do and maybe you don't. Now scat. I got company." Lily Joe's voice was gruff, but the shove she gave Abbey was more of a love pat.

"If I promise not to get 'dopted, will you let me bounce on your bed?"

"Yeah. Now scoot."

"What if they *make* me get 'dopted?"

"They better not," Lily Joe said as she tightened her hands into fists. "They just better not or I'll mur-der 'em!"

Abbey went skipping away singing, "Bouncity, bouncity, bounce if I want!"

Lily Joe picked up her bat with a sigh. "I s'pose I might as well tell you," she said, "somebody is tryin' to get Abbey. I always knew it would happen someday on account of her curly hair and all." She chewed her lower lip, and her nose got even pinker.

Jinky felt the tip of her own nose tingle in sympathy.

Lily Joe swiped her hand across her mouth. "On account of Abbey bein' my keep-sister, I get to have some say about her gettin' adopted, and I'm goin' to say plenty—against it!"

"What?"

"That's none of your business neither. I wish't I hadn't told you."

Jinky decided she had better try to change the subject; she'd never get to ask Lily Joe her question unless she got her into a better mood.

"Miss Weatherspoon's brother came home last night," Jinky offered.

"Yeah?" Lily Joe seemed to forget her troubles for a minute. "I'm glad he's back. Miss Carolina, she's the one stayin' with you-all, and Miss Virginia they need him somethin' awful. He ain't no murderer, I was just aimin' to scare your uppity sister."

"We know," Jinky said trying to ignore what Lily Joe called Molly. It was true, Molly had acted uppity, but Jinky didn't like somebody else saying so. "You help Miss Weatherspoon, don't you?" she asked.

"Sure, I help with the hospital, but they need their brother, too."

Now, Jinky thought, is my chance to ask about that hospital. "What do you *do?*"

"I thread needles—sew on heads even, if there's already holes to show where they go."

Heads? Holes? Jinky was more puzzled than ever. "What kind of a hospital is it, Pete's sake?"

"Doll hospital, course. What'd ya think? People send them dolls to fix from all over. Just for me helpin' out, they mend dolls for the little kids here and pay me besides."

A doll hospital! Jinky began to laugh.

"I don't see nothin' funny."

"Those boxes on their back porch, the ones marked 'heads' and 'bodies.' "

"They got heads and bodies in them. What did ya think? Miss Carolina, she says Miss Virginia can't tell one box from the other. And so she wrote it out plain for her. Miss Carolina's mighty particular about them heads. Don't want them scratched up or broken. She thinks dolls have got souls. Ha!"

"Molly and I thought—You see, we read a story once about two nice old ladies—Well, *I* didn't read it," Jinky admitted, digging her toe in the sand, "but Molly did and . . ." She shrugged. It didn't really matter now. "Say, why does Miss Car'lina wear her hat all the time?"

"Car-*o*-lina," Lily Joe corrected, and Jinky was reminded of Molly. "You-all better call her Car-*o*-lina or she gets mad. Says her papa named her after this state. He was real proud of this state and he wasn't fixin' for nobody to slur over its name."

"But why does she?"

"Her hat? That's to hide her hearing aid. Not that the contraption does any good, 'cause she can't hear nothing, even with it turned clear to the top. But she's plumb proud, and nobody dares ever say she wears it. Miss Virginia told me, and she said to keep still about it in front of her sister. And," Lily Joe added confidentially, "you-all better, too."

We're getting to be friends, Jinky thought. For some reason it made her feel important to be Lily Joe's friend. "Why don't you want Abbey to be adopted?" she dared to ask.

" 'Cause she's mine and I love her. I don't love nobody in this whole word 'cepting Abbey, and I'm not gonna' let nothing happen to her like happened to me." Lily Joe set her lips in a straight line and she whacked the sand with her ball bat. But this time Jinky knew it was somebody else Lily Joe was mad at, not her.

"What happened to *you?*" It was beginning to seem to Jinky that orphans led very exciting lives.

"I was fostered out."

Orphans also seemed to have a language of their own. "What's fostered out mean?"

"You know—foster parents. They hated me."

"Then why did they want to foster you?"

"So's they'd have somebody to hate, I reckon. Oh,

they liked me all right at first, but they had this kid of their own. Everything he done he went and told them I done. He started the hatin' in the first place. And I hated them back. If I was there now, I'd murder them all!"

"What did they do to you?" Jinky felt tingles of apprehension over the horrible things Lily Joe could probably tell.

She was shocked when, without warning, Lily Joe yelled at her, "Shut your mouth, you hear? You just shut up askin' so many snoopin' questions. They never done nothin' to me. Nothin'! Nothin'! Nothin'!"

"Lily Joe," Jinky pleaded, "my mother and father—"

Lily Joe whirled so fast Jinky thought she was going to whack her with the bat. "You jes' go back and tell your pa not to come snoopin' around here asking questions about me and making like he is tryin' to get me fostered out again. They ain't going to get me, and nobody ain't going to get Abbey!" Lily Joe burst into tears, threw her bat down, and ran.

Jinky ran after her. "Wait. Molly and I . . . we think . . . we're afraid that—"

Lily Joe stopped so suddenly that Jinky bumped into her, and when she did, Lily Joe began shoving and pushing Jinky toward the side yard of the orphanage. She gave one extra hard push, and Jinky lost her balance and fell headlong to the ground.

The fall hurt both Jinky's elbow and her pride. But it wasn't the hurt that made her start crying, it was because she was so mad. "All I wanted to do was ask you where you were born," she yelled up at Lily Joe.

"Born?" Lily Joe put her hands on her hips.

"That's all," Jinky assured her, getting to her feet and scrubbing off the tears. She plunged into her story before she lost her nerve. "Molly and I figured out that the folks have discovered there was a mix-up when we were babies—that Molly got mixed up with you, and that's why you and I look like twins."

Jinky paused and looked down at the ground. "Maybe we really *are* twins," she said, looking up again.

Lily Joe was laughing! "And here I thought your pa only took a shine to me because I looked like you," she hooted. "So that's it? They think I'm their own kid." She pointed at Jinky. "Well you can go back and tell them they're crazy." Then she cocked her head. "Where was this mix-up s'posed to have happened?"

"That's just it," Jinky said, rubbing her elbow. "*We* were born here in Nags Head."

"Well that proves it never happened," Lily Joe said, and her eyes lit up as if she had just thought of the best joke in the world, "because I was born smack in the middle of the Atlantic Ocean!" She doubled up with laughter.

What a whopper! Jinky thought. Just like her lie about Miss Weatherspon's brother. She must really be scared of getting fostered out to tell a whopper like that. Pete's sake, I suppose this means she was born right here and she's scared as we are about the mix-up.

Jinky wished she hadn't promised Molly she would ask. Molly would never believe such a lie. "Guess I better get going home," she said, ramming her hands into her pockets.

"Hey," Lily Joe told her, "soon's you get it all straightened out with your folks that there wasn't no mix-up—make sure they understand, you hear?—then you can come back whenever you want, but don't bring your sister. She don't like me and I don't like her."

Jinky nodded. In spite of Lily Joe's bad temper, and even though Lily Joe didn't like Molly, Jinky still couldn't help liking her. She supposed it was because inside she was blood-bound to Lily Joe—her real honest-to-goodness twin. Poor Molly, Jinky thought, poor brave Molly. She'll run away for sure now.

WHO IS LILY JOE?

All the way back home Jinky wished she hadn't gone to the orphanage. When I tell Molly what Lily Joe said about being born in the middle of the ocean, she thought, she'll know it's a lie. Molly will know that Lily Joe lied because she didn't want to admit she was born here same as we were.

I could tell Molly, Jinky thought, then stopped herself. No, I'm going to tell her the truth. I've learned one thing from Lily Joe, and that's if you tell lies *sometimes,* nobody believes you *ever.* I might have believed that whopper, no matter how impossible it sounded, if Lily Joe hadn't admitted she lied about Miss Weatherspoon's brother.

When Jinky reached home she found Duke and Baron stationed at the front door, and inside in the kitchen Miss Weatherspoon was humming noisily. Molly was nowhere in sight.

Jinky ran from room to room, downstairs then up, but no Molly.

She raced back outdoors to Pyewacket's box. The kitten was gone. Really anxious now, Jinky ran to the kitchen and asked Miss Weatherspoon if she knew where Molly was.

"She was here a while back. I told her not to go far, for there's weather brewing," Miss Weatherspoon assured Jinky with a shake of her hat brim.

Panic gnawed Jinky's stomach. Had Molly broken her promise and left already? No, Jinky decided, Molly was too honest for that. But where can she be?

There was no place left to look but the attic. Maybe Molly had gone up there to explore. Jinky bounded up the curving stairway, but she hesitated at the narrow door leading to the third floor. She thought of her vow never to go into the attic. She wished she could use that for an excuse, but she knew it was a vow that should be broken, since it was only a worry-wart vow.

Jinky started slowly up the attic stairway. As she climbed higher, the air grew hotter. The heat at the top almost burned Jinky's nose. She heard no sound except her own breathing.

The only light came from the one unboarded window at the end of the long slope-ceilinged room. From inside, the boarded window looked more than ever like an evil patch.

Jinky glanced cautiously around. There was an old spinning wheel with a broken foot treadle, stacks of books and magazines, and great bumpy mounds of something covered with dusty white cloth.

One mound was taller and skinnier than the rest. It looked as if a person could be hiding under it.

"M-Molly?" Jinky whispered into the hot silence. No answer. Gingerly, Jinky reached over and lifted the cloth to peep under. It was nothing but an old dress form that people use for sewing. "Fraidy-cat," she scolded herself.

The floorboards creaked under her feet as she tip-toed to the middle of the room and looked around. No Molly. Jinky had just turned back toward the steps when she heard a faint stir, a soft secret movement. She stopped dead still.

Another sound—a faint meow. Pyewacket! The mewing came from over near the windows. Jinky hurried toward them. There, curled up on some folded draperies, were Molly and Pyewacket. Molly was sound asleep. Little beads of perspiration lined her lips, and her damp hair curled on her forehead. The kitten stretched luxuriously and looked up at Jinky with innocent eyes. Then he settled again into the curve of Molly's arm.

Jinky saw Molly's diary lying open beside her. She picked it up quietly to see what Molly had written.

Dear Diary,
Since we arrived here Miss Weatherspoon's long-lost brother came home. Jinky found her real twin. She and Jinky look alike. They even walk alike, only Jinky talks much nicer. It is terrible to see two of the person you always thought was your very own twin, and to know you are not even sisters any more. If that girl was born the same place we were, I am going to run

away so nobody in our family will have to suffer by putting me in an orphanage. I will keep Pyewacket with me always.

Sincerely yours,
Molly Smith

As Jinky laid the diary back down, Molly stirred and opened her eyes. "I—I must have fallen asleep." She sat up quickly. "Tell me what happened."

"First of all," Jinky said, "I found out about Miss Weatherspoon's hosp—"

"First of all tell me where she was born!" Molly interrupted.

"Molly, it's a doll hospital. Those boxes had dolls' heads and bodies in them." Jinky saw Molly's eyes flicker with interest so she went on quickly, "And you'll never believe why she wears that hat!"

"*Where* was she born?"

"It's so no one will see her hearing aid. And somebody is trying to take Abbey away from the—"

"Jinky Smith, she *was* born in Nags Head!" Molly stood up and shook Jinky by the shoulders.

". . . and Lily Joe was crying because—"

Molly grabbed up Pyewacket. "I'm leaving."

"Molly, you can't! You promised to stay till the folks came back."

"I didn't promise exactly. I only said maybe I would stay or maybe I would leave when you got back from the orphanage. Now that we don't have to worry about Miss Weatherspoon any more, I'm going."

"Then I'm going with you." Jinky's nose wriggled miserably toward tears.

"Don't be silly," Molly stormed. "You have to stay here. You *belong* here."

Without really noticing, Jinky was aware that the attic had been getting darker and darker, and suddenly she heard the pelt of rain against the low roof. She looked up to see gusts of it blowing against the window. The storm Miss Weatherspoon had been predicting was here. "You can't go now," she cried, dizzy with relief. "It's raining."

"I'll go when it stops," Molly said and flounced toward the steps.

"Okay, when it stops you can." But even as Jinky said it, she didn't mean it, because a plan had come into the back of her mind. Molly would never leave without Pyewacket. She would steal Molly's kitten when Molly wasn't looking and take him— Where could she hide him so he couldn't be found?

The orphanage! She would run back to the oprhanage and get Lily Joe to hide the cat. Surely, if she could keep Molly here until the folks got home, they would stop her from running away. Of course she had promised not to tell the folks about Molly's plan of stowing away on a boat and living like Dick what's-his-name, but she'd think of something—once the folks came.

Maybe she would tell the folks right off that she and Molly knew about Lily Joe. Then they would realize how terrible Molly felt, and do *something* to make things right again.

As she followed Molly down the steps, Jinky wished she could think of a way to cheer her up. She

thought of telling Molly the meaning of the Indians'
secret password. Molly had always wanted to know.
Maybe if she knew what it meant, she could say it over
and over and get enough courage to go live close by
in the orphanage. That would be better than having
Molly in a foreign country.

But Jinky thought of her vow never to tell—not
even Molly—that "poohw raw" was "war whoop"
spelled backwards, and she wanted to keep this vow.
Anyway, she thought, no word in the world could
make it easy for Molly to live anyplace except with her
own family.

Jinky swiped at tears that rolled down her face.
Even if the folks *had* moved so they would be close
enough to see Molly every day, Molly's not living in
the very same house with them was a terrible thing.

Jinky swallowed hard as Molly put Pyewacket
down on her bed in their room. No matter how upset
Jinky was, she knew she had to keep that cat in sight.
It was her only chance of keeping Molly here.

"Molly," Jinky said with an ache in her throat, "I'm
sure if the folks do have to let you go to that orphanage they will hire a million detectives to get you back
out."

"They'll never put me there," Molly said angrily.
"They won't get the chance."

"I'd rather have you in the orphanage than clear
gone," Jinky cried. "I don't want Lily Joe for a twin.
I don't want a twin that's like me. I like having you for
my twin because you *are* different. I couldn't get

along without you. I wouldn't ever know what to do."

"It's going to be hard for me to get along without you, too, Jinky," Molly said and then added, "but we are both going to have to get used to it." She ran from the room.

Jinky started to follow, but remembered her plan. Now was the time. She snatched up Pyewacket from Molly's bed, tucked him under her roomy sweatshirt, and, making sure Molly was out of sight, sneaked down the stairs and out the front door.

The rain had practically stopped, and by the time Jinky reached the bridge the sun was out. Steamy vapors of moisture began to rise out of the sand as Jinky, carrying Pyewacket in her arms now, ran to the orphanage.

Once through the orphanage gate, she hurried back to the playground. It was deserted. Jinky quickly figured which window would be Lily Joe's and called her name as loud as she dared.

"Hey!" Lily Joe stuck her head out the window. "I'll be right down."

As soon as she saw the kitten, Lily Joe yelled, "You better get that dumb cat out of here."

Jinky looked around to be sure nobody had heard. "You have to do me a favor," she pleaded.

"What?" Lily Joe asked suspiciously.

"Hide this cat for me—just until tomorrow."

"Why should I?"

"I don't know, only please do!"

"Huh-uh." Lily Joe shook her head.

"This is a very valuable cat," Jinky said. "Something awful is going to happen to it if you don't help me." It was the truth. Pyewacket *was* valuable to Molly, and it would be awful if he and Molly ran away and probably starved to death.

"You know," Lily Joe said with a sly grin, "hiding the cat could be fun. Cats are against the rules here, and that might be one way to get even, on account of them tryin' to talk me into givin' up Abbey. Okay, I'll hide him for you."

Jinky handed Pyewacket to Lily Joe. "Take good care of him," she said, suddenly wondering if this was the right thing after all. "Where will you put him?"

"Down in the basement. Nobody hardly ever goes down there."

"What will they do to him if they find him?" Jinky whispered.

"They won't do nothin'. They wouldn't dare!" Lily Joe bragged. "I'm practically the boss around here. When I told them a while ago how I felt about Abbey gettin' adopted, the adopting folks and the supe agreed not to do it 'less I was ready. And I ain't never going to be ready. Those folks even agreed to come visit her twice a week and let her and me get to know them. They said even if they got to adopt her, which they won't, they won't take her off no further than where they live, Coquina Beach, over yonder." Lily Joe pointed with her thumb.

Then she said, almost as if she were talking to herself, "They was mighty nice people at that, and if it

wasn't for me lovin' Abbey so much, I might . . ."
Lily Joe's voice trailed off, and though Jinky hated to
leave, she remembered she had to get back as soon as
possible.

She told Lily Joe thanks and goodbye, took one last
look at Pyewacket, and hurried all the way back to the
Yaupon Moat house. She had just set one foot on the
rough boards of the bridge when she heard the familiar
chugging of Emmet Saunders' old car in the distance.
The folks were home at last!

Jinky dashed to the front door and yelled for Molly
to come quick. Both girls were waiting in the drive
by the time the car stopped. A huge feeling of relief
flooded over Jinky when she saw Father and Mother.
Molly was still here, even though she did look sad, and
Father looked a whole lot better.

After the kisses and hugs, Mother asked Molly to
run tell Miss Weatherspoon that Emmet Saunders was
waiting to take her into town.

Miss Weatherspoon must have had her belongings
ready, because she came hobbling right out carrying
her squat bag. As Jinky watched Miss Weatherspoon's
hat waving jauntily in the breeze, she thought about
Lily Joe saying Miss Weatherspoon believed dolls had
souls. Why, I almost *like* her, Jinky decided. If only
there wasn't this mix-up about Molly and Lily Joe, I
guess I'd be glad we moved here.

But there *was* the mix-up and Jinky moved closer
to Molly for fear, now that the folks were home, she
would vanish.

Father paid Miss Weatherspoon. Just before she climbed into the back seat of Emmet Saunders' car, the little old lady eyed Jinky and Molly sharply. "Now mind," she said, "that you two remember the difference between lanterns and beacons."

If only all this *would* turn out to be only lanterns, Jinky thought as she reached to help Father with the suitcases.

Father looked good as new. Mother looked rested and happy. They're back, Jinky thought, and Pyewacket is safely hidden from Molly. Those two things are beacons. But if something doesn't happen to save Molly, she vowed fiercely, I'll run away with her.

Father asked Jinky to take the overnight bags upstairs. When Jinky came back to the living room, she saw that only Father and Mother were there.

Molly was gone!

She's just looking for Pyewacket, Jinky assured herself shakily. But nevertheless, she felt relieved when Molly came running through the front door.

"Pyewacket's gone," Molly cried. "I can't find him anywhere!" Jinky could see that Molly was close to tears.

"Pyewacket?" Mother asked as she took off her jacket.

All at once Jinky thought of a way to let Mother and Father know that she and Molly knew about the secret. "He's at the *orphanage*," she said. "I asked Lily Joe to—"

"Orphanage?" Father demanded.

"Lily Joe?" Mother gasped.

Father let his pipe fall to his side. He and Mother exchanged the clothesline look. Though the look was hung with all kinds of startled thoughts, it definitely included both Molly and Jinky.

Surely, Jinky thought, *that's* a beacon!

"So you've seen her!" Mother cried. A little frown popped between her eyebrows. "Did you tell her who you are?"

Jinky could stand the suspense no longer. "Who *are* we?" she burst out. "I mean, *who is Lilly Joe?*" I mean, we *can't* let Molly—"

"Let's sit down," Mother said, looking at Father. "The time seems to have come to have a long talk."

THE GHOST VANISHES

Jinky sat down close to Molly on the red sofa. Molly's back was ramrod straight and her chin was lifted as if no matter what she heard she could stand it. But Jinky saw, out of the corner of her eye, that Molly's chin was quivering. She gave Molly's hand a little squeeze to let her sister know she would stick with her, no matter what.

Father rubbed his cane across his leg. "You girls already know," he said slowly, "that Jinky and Lily Joe look enough alike to be twins."

Jinky's heart pounded. Hearing Father say those words made them seem so . . . so *final*. She couldn't bear to look at Molly now, but kept her eyes on Father's serious face.

"The reason for this," Father went on, "is that Lily Joe is your cousin."

"*Cousin?*" Jinky and Molly cried at the same time.

"That's right," Father said.

Then everyone started talking at once.

"We thought—We were scared that—" Jinky began.

"Molly! What's the matter?" Mother rushed over to Molly, who had burst into tears.

"I thought she was Jinky's twin and I wasn't," Molly sobbed.

"Molly, Molly," Mother said softly.

"Here. Now. Everybody," Father broke in, "let's get this straight as quickly as we can. I'm sorry, Molly. Seems we have made a mistake keeping this from you girls."

"But we couldn't know—" Mother bit her lip as she patted Molly's cheek. "We were *told* this way would be best by the people who were trying desperately to help Lily Joe and—" Mother turned to Father. "Jim, you'd better start at the beginning of the story."

Cousin! Jinky was still thinking the word over and over to herself. No matter what the story was, it was bound to be good news now that she knew Lily Joe was only their cousin, and that Molly was still her very own twin. She looked at Molly, who was smiling at Father through her tears.

"Lily Joe is my own brother's child," Father explained. "Born after Joe was killed in the war. You see, several months ago an old war buddy of Joe's wrote me saying he had been trying to locate me for some time. He said there was a chance he might have information about a child, a relative of mine, a relative I had no idea even existed."

"Go on," Molly urged, scrubbing the tears from her eyes and beginning to look excited. Seeing Molly more like her old self made Jinky scrunch her shoulders with happiness.

"Well," Father continued, "before my brother Joe was shot down in a P-40 fighter plane over Germany, he married a girl from London, England, where his squadron was stationed. Her name was Lillian."

"Lillian! Joe!" Molly cried, clasping her hands around her knees. "Lily Joe is named after them both."

"That was the clue that led to our finding her," Father said. "But it all goes back to those terrible times eleven years ago, when London was being bombed every night.

"Lillian got word Joe had been killed. She was heartsick and frightened, worried about the life of her unborn baby. So, even though she expected the baby to be born any day, she boarded an English passenger ship to come to America, where they would both be safe."

Father stretched his legs to a more comfortable position, and Jinky stopped thinking about the story just long enough to be thankful he was better again.

"We knew," Father said, "that is, your Grandmother Smith and your mother here knew—I was in the war camp—they knew the ship Lillian was on was torpedoed. They knew Lillian was not among the survivors taken to Glasgow, Scotland. What they did not know was that Lillian's baby was born a few hours before the ship was attacked by our enemies. But Joe's buddy, who was on the same boat as Lillian, did know this."

So, Jinky thought, Lily Joe did not lie about where she was born! Jinky's head was spinning with all this news, but spinning happily. She smiled at Molly.

Molly smiled back and then asked Father, "And the detective?"

"After Joe's buddy contacted me, your mother and I hired Edward Scott to trace the survivors. He found that among them were several babies. All but one baby had been claimed by relatives during the years. That baby turned out to be Lily Joe.

"You see, Lillian had done her best to leave ways to identify her child in case of disaster. She had put a tiny bracelet made of tape around the baby's arm and printed the name Lily Joe on it.

"Then inside the baby's life jacket she had tucked a note that told their destination and undoubtedly also told the name of the baby's parents and grandmother."

"Our Grandmother Smith!" Molly exclaimed.

"But the salty ocean water washed away the writing except for the word Nags Head," Father said. "Eventually Lily Joe was brought to Nags Head by the American Red Cross."

So Lily Joe didn't lie about not having a last name, either, Jinky thought, or at least one she knew of. But it's Smith, same as ours!

"In the meantime," Father went on, "my mother

had died. She had a weak heart, and when she heard that Joe and Lillian were both dead, and that I was missing in action, it was too much for her."

Poor Father, Jinky thought. She watched his face closely and was glad when she saw it brighten as he said, "That's about all, except that the ship's log was lost at sea. Since it had contained the passengers' names, tracing them was even more difficult. After a time, the officials gave up trying to identify the baby named Lily Joe."

"Once we heard the name Lily Joe," Mother added, "we were almost certain she was ours. Then when Father came here to see her, and she looked so much like Jinky, there was no more doubt."

This reminded Jinky of another question. "Why didn't we just take Lily Joe out of the orphanage and bring her to live with us in Centerville?" she asked.

"That's the part we need your help with." Mother looked so earnest that Jinky and Molly both leaned forward.

"Through no fault of her own," Mother said sadly, "but because of some very unfortunate things that happened to her in a foster home, Lily Joe is not adoptable at the present time. And Jinky, from what the psychologist has told us so far, you and Lily Joe have a lot of the same interests. So, though it may be easier for you than for the rest of us to become her friend, it will also make some things harder for you."

Jinky nodded, remembering Lily Joe's outburst of that morning.

"You see," Mother said, "it is the orphanage's responsibility to be sure a child is physically and emotionally sound before—"

Molly whispered to Jinky, "That means she's nervous."

"More than nervous, Molly," Mother corrected. "She is emotionally disturbed. This means she cannot always control her own feelings. But we can help her, all of us, and the authorities at the Home are sure that with our help Lily Joe will soon be well enough to come and live with us for always. It will take time and lots of patience. But we *have* to succeed."

"I still don't understand why you didn't tell us about her," Jinky said.

"That was the big problem, Jinky. The people at the Home felt sure if Lily Joe could only know and trust us as her friends before she had to accept us as her family, she would adjust much quicker. Waiting to tell Lily Joe how much we want her to be part of our family was a hard decision to make—that and moving from our home—but a very fine doctor, as well as people at the orphanage who know her well, assured us this way was best."

"Are we still supposed to keep this a secret from Lily Joe?" Jinky asked.

"Yes," Mother said, "until she gets to know us better—until she thinks of us as friends."

I can make friends with her, Jinky thought, I can do that easy, because I like her. I *want* her for my friend. Suddenly the world seemed filled with beacons!

Jinky could hardly believe she had heard right when Molly said, "I could try to be more like Jinky, because I think Lily Joe already likes *her*."

"No," Mother objected. "To pretend to be something we aren't would only be fooling her and would confuse her more."

"You could ask her if you could go to Miss Weatherspoon's doll hospital and help mend dolls with her," Jinky suggested. "You're good at sewing and so is Lily Joe."

"That's a perfect idea." Molly sounded grateful. She turned to Mother. "You mean Lily Joe should learn to like each one of us for what we are, even if we are different than she is?"

Mother smiled for the first time since they started talking about Lily Joe. "That's right, Molly dear."

Jinky thought about that a minute. And that's why I couldn't stand to lose Molly, she decided. I *do* like her for the way she is, and I guess, Pete's sake, I guess I even like myself for the way I am, too.

Everything had been explained except the telegram Emmet Saunders brought the night Jinky eavesdropped on the stairs. Jinky still wondered about that, and even though it brought up her bad habit she decided to ask.

"Edward Scott had been trying to find out if Lily Joe had any relatives left in England," Father answered Jinky's question. "The people at the orphanage also told us we needed to provide as complete a family as possible for Lily Joe to identify with. But the telegram said he found no one. We, here in this room, are all the family she has."

"But we're enough!" Jinky cried. "I'm just sure we're enough." She saw the wonderful clothesline look pass between Mother and Father. Then Mother looked around the living room. "My, it's good to be home," she said with a sigh.

Home? The word took Jinky by surprise. She thought about how unsure and frightened she'd been when they first came into this house. And how, later, she'd been afraid of Miss Weatherspoon, and her brother, and even those silly boxes. Pete's sake, she sure had mistaken plenty of lanterns for beacons.

Jinky thought about the night she'd watched Mother standing by the window, and how sure she'd been that it was a ghost Mother was talking about when she said, "Now that I know she's out there some-where, so close, I'm almost afraid."

But then Jinky smiled inside herself, because there really had been a ghost here. Not the ghost of Virginia Dare roaming silently over the sand dunes at mid-night, but the ghost of the third twin.

The third-twin ghost was one she and Molly had made real by believing in it the way Miss Weather-spoon said.

Now that Jinky knew Molly really was her twin, that ghost, like all proper ghosts, had vanished in thin air.

And, in its place it had left a very real third twin—their brand-new cousin, Lily Joe.